STEAMED

Steamed

A Maid in LA Mysteries

Holly Jacobs

Ilex Books 2018
ISBN-13: 978-0-9992736-5-4
ISBN-10: 0-9992736-5-5

For Pam Hanson, You've been a wonderful, supportive friend for years and I love that you love my singing...well, at least when you hear it through a thick wall! You've been a fun and super talented writing partner. And now you're my editor. I'm a very lucky woman!

For Dee J. Adams, a great friend, a great writer...and a nice LA Connection! Any mistakes about LA or Hollywood are all mine, and let's pretend they're not really mistakes but rather artistic license! And a very big thanks for suggesting the "Mortie."

TABLE OF CONTENTS

Dear Reader,

I know you're accustomed to seeing my books set in Erie, or nearby cities. But this story needed to be set in LA. I mean, there aren't too many award winning television writers in Erie. I've had fun visiting LA with this book. (You'll still find an Erie connection!)

I'm so very excited about Quincy Mac. She's one of those characters I've had in mind for years. She's simply been waiting her turn. Quincy's a mom. She's a business owner ... she's a maid. She's also the family's black sheep. She's a character I can identify with on so many levels. I'm a mom. And you can consider my writing a business, so I'm technically a business owner. And since I am a mom, I'm sort of a glorified maid ... well, actually, there's not much glory in it. As for being a black sheep, well, I might not be a maid in a family full of doctors, but I am the girl who grew up with her nose in a book ... and now writes them for a living. My family and friends have been known to give me an odd look or two (see the reviews that follow), and there have definitely been a few head-shakes and shoulder-shrugs in my general direction.

I so hope you enjoy Quincy and her friends.

When you're done, check out **Dusted: A Maid in LA Mystery**. It's out now!

Holly

REVIEWS FOR STEAMED:

"Hey, at least it's not a romance." Holly's son.

"Dear God, not another cop character. Any police procedural inaccuracies are all Holly's. They are not the fault of her personal police models. Of course, the fact that she portrays cops as hunks is totally accurate." Holly's husband and two brothers (aka her cop models)

"Holly is a fantastic writing talent... not that I'm biased." ~Holly's favorite daughter*

"Holly Jacobs is an auto-buy for me. Not that I buy her books... she gives them to me." ~Holly's favorite daughter*

"Holly makes me laugh... so do her books." ~Holly's favorite daughter*

DISCLAIMER: Holly has three daughters...she has no favorites.

"Holly always had a vivid imagination... but I never thought it would lead her to think up innovative ways to kill people. She sure knows how to make a mother proud!" ~Holly's mom

CHAPTER ONE

WHEN I MOVED TO LA, I was an eighteen year old with stars in my eyes. Well, not exactly in my eyes, but rather *on* my eyes. My high school best friend bought me sunglasses with lenses shaped like stars for when I *Made It*. Lottie always said the words in such a way you just knew they were capitalized.

Made It.

Yes, I graduated from high school and moved to LA. I planned to be a famous actress. Lottie made me promise I'd wear my star-shaped glasses on my first Oscar red carpet walk. My goal was to take Hollywood by storm.

These days, those glasses are in a drawer in my bedroom and I have two much smaller goals. One is that I want to wear my jeans without a muffin-top. After three kids, I'd developed a bit of a baby-pooch that wants to creep out above the waistband of my jeans. I longed for the days when pants had waistbands that were higher. Back then you could tuck your baby-pooch in. These days your options are exercise, wear Spanx, or learn to suck it in.

I tend to suck it in ... when I remember.

My second goal is an empty nest.

It's not that I don't love my boys. I do. I have three sons—Hunter, Miles and Eli. They are eighteen, seventeen and sixteen. I've been a parent practically my entire adult

1

life. I'm ready for a time when I simply have to worry about me and no one else.

This summer is my trial empty-nest.

The boys left last night to spend four weeks in the Bahamas with their father and his most recent wife, Peri.

Now, my place isn't exactly a dump, but compared to their dad's house, my three-bedroom bungalow in the out-of-the-way neighborhood of Van George is a cardboard box in some alley.

And while thirty-eight isn't exactly over-the-hill, next to Peri, the twenty-year-old, I am ancient.

I miss my boys (and I realize the irony in longing for an empty nest, but missing them when they're on vacation). I try not to mind when my ex takes the boys on fabulous vacations—and most of the time I don't mind—but getting ready for work in a quiet house, I minded.

My ex, movie producer Jerome Smith, is a nice guy...a nice guy with a taste for younger women. Specifically women between the ages of twenty and twenty-five. The exact ages I married, then divorced him. Or rather, he divorced me.

Jerome had two marriages before me, and three marriages since, all within those same parameters. His current wife's my favorite. I really like Peri despite the way her breasts perk and mine just sort of...well, hang loosely if they're not strapped down. I think Peri sort of appeals to my maternal instincts. I don't have a daughter.

Maybe I'll adopt her when Jerome divorces her.

TGIF, I told myself. I'm thirty-eight, and until the boys come home from their summer visit with their father, I'm footloose and fancy-free.

Maybe it isn't exactly the life I'd dreamed of when I moved to LA, but it's a good life.

Oh, sometimes I still wish that I were starring in some movie of the week instead of heading into Mac'Cleaners.

Yes, that's right—I no longer have stars in or on my eyes. Rather than achieving stardom, I have three sons and clean houses for a living. It's honest work, and it's flexible enough that when I was younger I could take time off and go on auditions. Now that I'm part owner and thirty-eight, I don't go to many auditions.

Okay, so I haven't been on an audition in five years—I've discovered that I'm a size twelve girl in a size two world.

I missed the fame and fortune boat.

Okay, so I could live without fame or fortune, if only I could figure out what I wanted to do with my life sometime before menopause hit. Owning a business keeps the boys and me afloat financially but lately, I'd had a feeling that it was time for a change. The kids weren't such kids anymore. Hunter would start college in the fall.

That empty nest is just around the bend. Soon I'll be able to live my own life.

And I know I want something more.

I'd said I wanted to act since I was six. I never gave any thought to doing something else. But it's clear that acting isn't going to be my ultimate career.

So while I wait to figure out what I want to do, I clean houses. I need to figure out soon because I'll be turning forty in a couple years. Forty sounds so very grown up, and grown-ups should have some idea about the direction they want their lives to take.

But I wasn't going to think about direction today.

Today, I was going to get my work done and then go do something decadent.

I'd like to say I was planning to go to a bar and pick up guys—well at least pick up a guy—but I'll probably end up going to the store and picking up Ben and Jerry's, then head home and try and catch up on all the chick-flicks the boys make me miss.

Feeling a bit better, I walked into the small brick storefront that was only a mile from my house. It proudly proclaimed Mac'Cleaners on the plate glass window with a tartan weaving through the letters. I walked through the small reception room and back to my partner, Tiny's office.

Big mistake.

There's nothing worse than starting the day as a single, directionless, mother of three and then walking into the middle of the wonderful world of weddings.

Tiny's marrying Salvador Mardones in September. September 30th to be exact. And she's going slightly insane...a bit further over the brink each day.

"Tiny?" I called, hoping she was somewhere in the sea of tulle and satin.

"I'm here, Quincy," she said from the back corner.

Tiny's not very... tiny that is. She's five eight and looks like a model. Skin the color of strong tea and dark hair with a tendency to curl. She's gorgeous and simply a beautiful soul. We make an interesting pair, what with me having Irish fair skin, a light sprinkling of freckles that might have been cute when I was in my teens, but aren't as much when at thirty-eight. And my hair... well, it was blond when I moved to LA thanks to Lottie and Miss Clairol. These days, it has gone back to its brownish roots...literally.

Tiny smiled as I walked in, and I couldn't muster up true annoyance that her smile was messing with my grouchy mood because she radiated happiness. The kind of happiness I knew she deserved.

"It's getting worse, isn't it?" she asked, gesturing at her office.

I surveyed the room. "Yeah."

"I just can't help myself. I want this wedding to be perfect because Sal's perfect."

Truth is, Sal is perfect. He's my five five height, balding and has a beer belly that makes my small baby-pooched stomach look like washboard abs.

But he's truly one of the nicest guys in the world.

Tiny had a history of dating losers. But that was over because Sal … well, he's a winner.

"The wedding will be perfect," I promised.

I'd see to it, even though I'd rather have wisdom teeth pulled than plan a wedding this elegant.

Me, if I ever get married again, I'm eloping. Something fast and simple. Someone saying the official words, then my new husband and me back at some hotel having sex. Lots and lots of sex.

It had been a while, which might explain why my mind skipped right over finding Mr. Right and a wedding and went right to the sex.

"Speaking of help," Tiny said slowly, "we need some today. Theresa's out."

Rats.

"It's my turn, isn't it?" I asked, though I knew the answer.

She nodded.

When one of our employees calls in sick, we take turns filling in.

Today it was my turn to fill in.

I should have just gone back to bed this morning.

Grumbling to myself, I left Tiny to hold down the fort and took Theresa's folder for the day. The nice thing about working outside the office is that the day always went fast.

Today was no exception. By three in the afternoon, I was on my way to the last job.

As soon as I finished Mr. Banning's, I'd decided that I was going shopping for a new pair of shoes rather than Ben and Jerry's.

More money, less calories.

I thought the trade-off was worth it.

On a day like today, I didn't just want new shoes—I needed them. So, I grabbed Mr. Banning's printout from Theresa's folder. I was anxious to finish this last job.

Mr. Banning's was a BWP/wL.

A basic-weekly-pickup, with laundry.

I knocked on his door, even though the file said the odds of him being home at three o'clock in the afternoon were slim to nil.

I used our key and let myself in. I surveyed the living room with disgust. There was nothing basic about this job.

The place was a mess.

I mean, a real pigsty. Worse than my boys' rooms…and that's saying something. Teenage boys are very toxic.

Mr. Banning was a whole new level of toxicity, though. Underwear was hanging from a chandelier, empty glasses and plates were scattered through the room.

Oh, geesh. Mr. Banning had a Mortie. All TV Network, ATVN, had begun to hand out the award ten years ago and it had quickly become one of the premier Hollywood awards.

Hey, I might not be an actual actress, but I know stuff.

I noticed not out of some sort of awe that I was cleaning a Mortie winner's home, but rather because the award was sitting in the middle of the leather couch, covered in something. Maybe someone had dipped it into some of the food. Ugh. It looked like they'd tried to wipe it off before throwing it on the couch, but they didn't wipe hard enough.

To top it off, there were footprints on the light beige carpet. Big footprints. Whoever wore those shoes had really big feet. Thankfully, there were only two. As if whoever made the prints realized they'd tracked in mud and took off their shoes, because those two prints were it.

Well, there'd been at least one considerate person.

I tried to make a mental list of how best to approach this job.

In the end, there was nothing to do but start. I gathered dishes and cups and the pots and pans in the kitchen and had the dishwasher running minutes later. I even hand-washed the Mortie—which was about as heavy as a bag of sugar, heavier than I'd thought the old-fashioned silver television would be—and gave it a thorough polish. When I was done, the inscription on the silver television screen really stood out. Steve Banning. *Dead Certain.*

I remembered that show. It was a comedy about a medical examiner's office.

I set the Mortie on the mantle, thinking that was a more appropriate place for it than the couch.

There was a desk next to the fireplace. It had an old relic of a computer on it. The keyboard's cord dangled over the edge of the desk. Yeah, that wasn't going to work well.

I plugged the keyboard into the back of the tower.

Next, I dragged a garbage can around the room and made short order of the rest of the mess.

I debated whether I should toss the chandelier's panties out, but opted to put them in the wash with a load of clothes. At least when Mr. Banning returned them to whoever they belonged to, they'd be clean.

Maybe they belonged to him?

The thought was enough to make me decide to concentrate on the job at hand rather than on the underclothing our Mortie-winning client wore.

There was a small steam-cleaner in the back of the Mac'Cleaners van. It made short work of the footprints. I worked on the laundry as I vacuumed and dusted. By then the dishwasher was finished, so I unloaded it then cleaned the kitchen.

I found the bra that matched the panties under the sink.

Personally, I didn't want to know why there was a bra under the sink. Maybe Mr. Banning had a dishwashing fetish and the mystery naked woman helped him out? The mental image was disturbing.

I knew walking into the place that Mr. Banning liked women.

It said so on his file. Right after BWP/wL it said *DOG*.

That's our code for he liked women a lot and liked a lot of them.

Yes, Mr. Banning is a dog…a letch.

But he never bothers the staff, so it didn't bother us.

Mac'Cleaners is an equal opportunity employee. We stake our reputation on good service and discretion.

This job was going to require a lot of discretion on my part. I wondered if Theresa's illness had anything to do with knowing that Mr. Banning's place was this bad and that she'd have to clean it up?

Kitchen done, I moved onto and finished the bathroom as well. Then I folded a load of laundry and put another one in the dryer. With the job almost done, I was getting excited about shoe shopping, which in LA is a unique treat. So many shoes, so few feet. I headed to Mr. Banning's bedroom.

If his living room was a pit, I really didn't want to know what condition his bedroom was in. Knowing that all that stood between me and some Santee Alley bargain shopping was this bedroom, I opened the door, took all of one step in and…screamed.

It wasn't a frustrated scream.

It wasn't even a this-guy-is-such-a-pig sort of scream.

No, it was more like a there's-a-bloody-dead-body-on-the-bed sort of scream.

Loud, long and more than a little crazed.

I wanted to keep screaming and run right out of the house, but I managed to get myself under control. The killer had to be long gone, or else he—or she—would have attacked me as I cleaned. I was safe. I couldn't say the same for poor Mr. Banning.

I reached in my back pocket, pulled out my cell phone and called 911.

"You've reached Los Angles emergency dispatch."

"I need help," I blurted out.

"What is the nature of your emergency?" the man on the other end of the phone asked.

"Mr. Banning's dead. There's blood on his head and his eyes are open."

Those eyes were going to give me nightmares for the rest of my life.

"Your address ma'am?"

"I'm at, he's at—" I had to think a moment, but then I somehow pulled his address from the fog that was my mind and blurted it out.

"Who are you?" the operator asked.

"I'm the maid. Quincy Mac."

Now, some people prefer the term domestic engineer, or some fancy title. I call it like I see it. I'm a maid.

I had no idea why I thought of what to call myself at that moment. Maybe it was nerves. After all it's not every day I find a dead client.

Thinking about my job description was easier than thinking about those eyes and all that blood.

"Ma'am are you sure he's dead?"

"I don't think there's any way someone could look that bloody and blue and still be breathing."

This was the ultimate topper to my day from hell.

A dead man in the bedroom.

As I talked to the operator, I walked outside. Not really walked, trotted. I moved fast. I mean, no way was I staying in a house with a dead guy.

I was thankful for my cell phone as I stepped out onto the bright sidewalk.

Perfect.

All that LA sunshine made it hard to believe that someone was dead a short distance away.

The emergency operator continued asking me questions. The company's name, my name and address, etc...

Personally, I sort of zoned out. I think I answered him all right but couldn't be sure.

Actually, I didn't want to be sure.

I just wanted to go home.

The police arrived, followed by an ambulance. They stopped and talked to me a minute, then hurried off to check on Mr. Banning.

I wondered how long I had to wait around.

I wanted to go home now.

I mean, I didn't even want to hunt for the perfect pair of bargain shoes or stop for Ben and Jerry's. That just shows how hard I'd been hit by this.

Anytime a woman passes up Ben and Jerry's or new shoes...well, it's moved beyond a bad day and turned into a found-a-dead-body-on-the-bed sort of day.

I was wondering if I could just sneak out. The authorities had my information already, so they didn't need me. But then *He* walked up to me.

He was tall, lean and oh-so-yummy. Dark hair with just a touch of grey at the temples.

Not one of LA's boy-toys who are a dime a dozen.

No, this was a real man walking toward me like some hero out of a movie.

Maybe he was here to take me away from all this.

Maybe he'd seen me from across the street looking fragile, yet still beautiful.

Okay, so beautiful was a bit unattainable. I'd settle for fragile and cute. Yeah, I could pull off cute on a good day and I felt very, very fragile at the moment.

Ah, my hero.

I sucked in my baby-pooch, pulled out my old acting class skills and concentrated on looking even more fragile and cute. It worked. He walked right up to me, shot me a concerned look, then ... he flashed a badge.

I realized that his concerned look was more of an assessing look.

My hero was a cop.

Okay, so maybe *He* was a cop who was concerned because I looked so fragile?

"Ma'am? You're," he flipped open his little notepad in a very Adam-12 sort of way, and that particular mental-analogy really dated me I realized morosely as he finished, "Quincy Mac?"

"Yes." I thought about fluttering my eyelashes but decided to give up before I embarrassed myself.

"You're the one who found Mr. Banning and called 911?"

"Yes." I wanted to say more, so much more. But even a gorgeous knockout cop couldn't make me forget I'd just found a dead body, at least not for long. And thoughts of Mr. Banning, sitting on his bed, covered in blood with his eyes open, well, that sort of froze the words in my throat.

"The officer over there said that the house has been pretty much wiped clean."

I had professional pride in my job well done. "Not *pretty much*, all the way. Other than the bedroom, which I didn't clean for obvious reasons."

The cop quirked his eyebrow. "He said the bedroom was wiped clean as well."

I think the hunky cop just called me a liar.

Actually, I didn't just think it—I could see it in his eyes. The man actually thought I'd gone into a room with a dead body in it and cleaned it up?

My attraction to him slipped more than just a notch. It evaporated.

"Not by me," I assured him. "I took one look at the body on the bed, called 911 as I got the heck out of there. I guarantee that I didn't stop to clean the room first."

"But you admit you cleaned the rest of the house?" the cop asked.

"Of course I admit it. I'm the maid. That's what they pay me to do. Don't you think that if I'd have known someone had died, I'd have simply called the cops first? If you'd seen what a state the house was in when I arrived, you'd know I'd have welcomed an excuse not to clean it. But I did clean it and I did a fine job of it."

Cleaning houses is an honest profession. I might have been a bit befuddled, but even in my present state I wasn't going to let some cop make me feel less than the professional that I am.

He didn't answer my question. He simply asked, "And the other officers said there were footprints you steamed off the carpet?"

"Yes. I'm good at what I do. When Mac'Cleaners cleans a house, it's totally clean."

"Ma'am, the coroner says that Mr. Banning probably died sometime last night." He paused a moment and sort of gave me a hard stare with his charcoal grey eyes.

That stare did things to me … my knees felt rather weak and my heart rate sped up. I don't think it was shock.

Lust.

That's what it felt like.

I hadn't had a good case of lust in a while. But I was pretty sure that I remembered how if felt and this was it.

"Quincy," he said, soft and low.

Yes, I wanted to say.

Oh, yes.

I've read that when someone experiences death they want to make love just to prove they're still alive, to prove that they can still feel something.

I think my lust for this cop went deeper than just a need to prove I was alive. It might have been a need to prove I still had a libido, but mainly I think it had something to do with a long, hard orgasm.

I was almost forty and I'd read enough magazine articles to know that meant I was reaching my sexual prime.

Only it had been a long time since I'd been primed.

This guy was making remember how much I enjoyed a good priming.

"Yes," I said out loud. Hoping he'd say, *let's forget about the dead body and get you home to bed.*

Oh, yeah. I wanted him to tuck me in, and then tuck himself right next to me.

Naked.

"Quincy," he said again, "by any chance you have an alibi for last night?"

"An alibi?" I squeaked, all lust-filled thoughts fleeing from my head.

Alibi?

Rats.

I knew what that meant.

I watch *Law and Order*, *Law and Order SVU*, and *Law and Order Criminal Intent*. Is that all? I might be forgetting one, but that's understandable, given my circumstances.

Oh, and I watch *CSI*.

All that television meant I knew that cops didn't ask witnesses for alibis.

They asked suspects for them.

I was a murder suspect.

CHAPTER TWO

AFTER CONFESSING THAT I didn't have an alibi, super cop—who finally had introduced himself as Detective Parker—let me go with a warning not to leave town.

I felt like a teenager who'd been grounded.

Grounded to the city of Los Angeles.

I'd lost the desire for shopping or ice cream, and I couldn't face my empty, messy house, so I went back to the office to find Tiny.

She'd know what to do.

Tiny was levelheaded, plus she had Sal.

Sal, in addition to being perfect, was a lawyer.

Okay, so he did a lot of corporate, paper sort of law, but still, he had to have some idea what I should do next.

"Quincy," Tiny said, excitement in her voice as I hurried into her office, "You'll never believe what I did today—"

She stopped short, gave me one long look, then hurried forward, leaned down and wrapped me in her arms.

Tiny didn't let go as she asked, "What happened?"

"My last stop of the day…the man, a Mr. Banning?" I paused, hardly able to bring myself to think the words much less say them.

"Mr. Banning?" Tiny prompted. Her voice sounded very concerned, as if she knew something terrible had happened by some sort of best-friend ESP.

We were that close. Closer than I'd been to Lottie in high school, and Lottie and I had practically lived in each other's back pockets.

Tiny and I were even closer. We knew things without being told.

I pulled back and said, my voice barely a whisper, "He was... dead."

"Dead?" she asked weakly, pulling us both onto the couch. "Dead?"

"Not just dead... murdered. And the cops think I'm a suspect. I'm grounded to LA until further notice."

"You?" she asked weakly. "You're a suspect? Why would they think you killed him?"

"It seems I cleaned up all the evidence."

"You what?" She shook her head. "Okay start at the beginning. No wait," she said before I could utter a word. "You don't want to tell this more than once. Let me call Sal, then tell us both the whole story."

Sal's office was conveniently located just across the street. That's how he and Tiny had met, bumping into each other day after day.

One morning the bumping led to smiles, then the smiles led to morning greetings, then eventually those morning exchanges led to a coffee and coffee... well it led to their upcoming wedding.

"Yeah. Call Sal," I said. "That would be good."

I'd known I could count on Tiny.

Ten minutes later I spilled out the whole story. Tiny and Sal, being such good friends, didn't interrupt or pepper me with questions. They just sat quietly and listened.

Just listened.

A true friend is the kind of person who can simply listen to you tell a macabre tale like mine and not interrupt. Not exactly a greeting-card sentiment. *Good friends don't interrupt when you talk about the dead body in the bedroom.* No, I doubt they'll make one of those, but if they do, I'd buy it for Tiny and Sal.

"Oh, Quincy, I'm so sorry," Tiny said softly.

I felt better having shared it all.

And I felt better yet when Tiny gave me another hug.

"So what do you think, Sal?" I asked. "Am I in trouble?"

He was seated across from us in Tiny's desk chair. He leaned over, took my hand and gave it a quick squeeze as he offered me a reassuring smile. "I think the police are just being thorough. They'll need to check out your story, but you didn't kill him, so you're fine. And you had no way of knowing you were cleaning up a murder scene so I can't even begin to think of anything they could charge you with. If they tried *accidental cleaning*, the D.A. would laugh them out of his office."

"So, you think I'm okay?" I wasn't so sure. "My Uncle Bill spent two years in prison because the cops said he robbed a local market. He didn't. But he spent those two years behind bars anyway."

I didn't want to spend two years behind bars until they figured out the truth.

I had three sons.

Granted, they were older now, but they still needed me, even if they didn't need me as much as they once had. Jerome was a weekend and summer sort of dad at best. He'd never handled the day-to-day boy stuff. And his latest wife was practically a teenager herself. Peri would never be able to cope with my three.

Oh, they're good boys, but they need discipline.

I simply didn't think their father and stepmother were up to the task.

Plus, there were graduations and proms to witness. Embarrassing pictures to take. There were birthdays and holidays.

Thinking about all I might miss out on, I felt more and more morose.

"I simply can't go to jail," I declared, as if saying it out loud would make it so.

No, I couldn't go to jail because I cleaned the wrong house on the wrong day. I'd never done anything in my life to warrant that kind of karma. Okay, there was that whole Allie Mays incident in high school, but even that didn't warrant dead-body karma.

"It will be fine," Sal assured me.

I wasn't so sure I could afford to believe him.

I wasn't sure I could trust the cops to find out the truth. Oh, they eventually figured out my Uncle Bill didn't rob that market, but he spent those two long years in jail anyway.

He got a tattoo.

My father was so embarrassed that his brother had a tattoo. His twin brother. No one in the Mac family had ever gone to jail or permanently disfigured themselves on purpose.

The Mac family had high standards.

They were doctors.

Every last one of them.

My parents, my older brothers, even my grandparents...on both sides.

They were all doctors except Uncle Bill and me.

We were the black sheep in my white-coat-wearing family. I cleaned houses and Uncle Bill was an ex-con with a tattoo. I might be used to being a black sheep, but I didn't want to go to prison and get a tattoo in order to become any blacker.

My skin wasn't as tight as it used to be, and at thirty-eight I knew it would be getting looser by the year. What if I spent decades in jail?

I'd come out saggy, pruned-up and sporting a wrinkled tattoo. "I just can't go to jail," I said again just to be sure Tiny, Sal and the universe understood that jail wasn't going to happen.

"Oh, honey, there's no way you're going to jail," Tiny said, giving me another hug.

Sal patted my knee. "They let you go, after all. They'll do some checking and find out you had nothing to do with the murder. You have no motive. You'll be in the clear. This will all be over before the boys get home from their summer vacation."

I wanted to believe them both.

Really wanted to.

But I was left with a sinking feeling that this was trouble.

Big trouble.

Sal and Tiny wanted me to stay with them, but I just wanted to go home and pretend that this day hadn't happened.

I assured them I was fine—that Sal had made me feel better.

In fact, the only thing that was going to make me feel really better was if the cops found the real killer.

I got home and looked at the mess the boys had left as they packed for their vacation.

I should have cleaned it up last night, but I was exhausted from getting the boys out the door with their dad. I'd thought I'd clean tonight. Normally the mess would be driving me nuts. But nothing was normal today and I just couldn't bring myself to start. It felt like too much of an effort.

Instead, I kicked a bunch of the boys' clothes off the couch, pulled out an afghan and curled up under it.

I felt cold, despite the fact it was August in LA.

I spotted the remote under a blue sweatshirt and turned on the television.

It was a news report.

And there, behind the reporter was Mr. Banning's house.

"... Steve Banning was a respected Hollywood insider. His credits include his Mortie award-winning television series, *Dead Certain*, as well as ..." The reporter rattled off an impressive list of shows and movies that I recognized. He ended with, "... Mr. Banning was found by a maid this afternoon. The police said they have a preliminary list of suspects and are confident they'll have the murderer in custody soon."

How could they have a list of suspects already? It had only been a couple hours. I know they'd talked to me. But could they have interviewed anyone else?

Not likely.

Visions of tattoos flashed in my mind.

Maybe it wouldn't be too bad if I picked a pretty tattoo. Maybe a unicorn ... a symbol of purity and innocence. I pictured a wrinkled, pruned unicorn and decided that wasn't the way to go.

So, there was no option. I couldn't go to jail. No way I was going to let the cops pin a murder on me just because I'm good at my job.

Quincy Mac was not going to be a patsy.

Their fall guy.

Fall-woman.

I wasn't like my uncle, willing to wait to be cleared. I was going to clear myself.

But how?

Thoughts of all those Law and Orders, *CSI* and *Castle* flashed through my mind. Oh, too bad I didn't have Nathan Fillion, aka Rick Castle, here helping me out like the cops did in *Castle*. Yes that wisecracking author and pseudo-detective would be on the case. He'd prove my innocence by dinner.

Since I didn't see Mr. Fillion knocking on my door, I'd simply have investigate Mr. Banning's murder myself. I'd prove I didn't do it. Yes, in order to save myself, it looked as if I was going into the private investigator business.

Okay, so where did I start?

I'd never hunted for a murderer before.

Paper. I'd start a file. It seemed to me all the best cops on televisions had files. *Hand me the file on the Banning case,* one would say to the other, and a manila folder would be tossed across the desk.

I went back into my bedroom and rooted through the desk until I found an old manila folder that one of the boys had used for a report. It said *Oral Hygiene* on the tab.

I scratched the words out and wrote *Banning* across the tab. I had to write small because the crossed out Oral Hygiene took up most of the space.

But I felt rather official.

I was investigating a case. Quincy Mac, Private Detective. I even had a file. Of course there was nothing in it.

I wonder if Matlock started out like this? Remington Steele. Now, there was another great television detective … very pretty to look at, as well. I love Pierce Brosnan.

I realized that fantasizing about fictional detectives and their real-life actor counterparts wasn't going to solve this case, but I didn't have any better ideas.

I went back to the couch, sat down and stuffed some loose-leaf paper in the file. It wasn't empty any more. Of course, I hadn't written anything on any of the loose-leaf. I didn't know what to write.

The phone rang.

I picked it up—an automatic response—and wished I hadn't. I didn't want to talk to anyone. But I said, "Hello?"

"Hi, Mom it's Miles."

Miles. My boy.

He was off having fun, not realizing his old mom was headed to jail for a murder she didn't commit. She'd come out a few decades in the future with her wrinkly unicorn tattoo and a felony murder conviction following her around.

My eyes started to itch and my nose sort of tingled.

"Hi, sweetie," I said, my voice sounding sort of oddly flat. I forced some pep into it as I asked, "Are you guys having fun?"

"Sure. We're teaching Peri how to scuba dive."

"That's nice." Nice boys. My boys were so very nice. And now they'd have to live with the stigma of having a mother convicted of murder.

I looked for something to wipe my nose on and found a napkin by last night's pizza box.

"So what's new with you?" Miles asked.

I couldn't tell him, I'm officially a suspect in a murder and grounded to the city of LA. So, I settled for, "You know me, same old, same old."

"Mom, you've got to get out and live it up a bit. You're single for the next month. Single in LA. Go out and do something crazy."

"Crazy," I murmured. Crazy like investigating a murder? "Sure, honey, I will," I promised honestly.

"Good. We'll call every couple days," he promised. "I just wanted to be sure you were okay. I know you miss us when we're gone."

"I do, but I'm fine. Don't worry about me and just have fun."

"You, too. I mean it, Mom. Do something different. Shake your life up a bit. Love you." He hung up.

He'd said *love you*. Would he still love his tattooed convicted murderer mother?

He wanted me to shake up my life? I started to shake again, and pulled the afghan close around me, clutching the not-quite-so-empty file folder to my chest.

My boys. They'd be home in a month not knowing they'd be coming home to a mother on death row.

Hey, wait a minute. Did California have a death row? I was sick that I didn't know the answer to that. What kind of person doesn't know if their state has a death penalty?

Now, Texas has a death penalty, but I couldn't think of another state that did. I'm sure there are death-penalty states as well. I should know which ones were.

I should lobby against them, especially if I was going to be on death row. Okay, so maybe then it would be a conflict of interest.

Once I cleared up this whole suspicion-of-murder thing, I was going to be a better citizen. I'd get active in politics. I was going volunteer on someone's campaign—an honest politician with integrity if I could find one. I'd know things about California's penal system.

There was a whole world of things I was going to try and do.

But first I had to find out…who killed Mr. Banning? So, where did someone start an investigation like that?

Talk to the witnesses.

But I was the only witness I knew of and I hadn't witnessed the crime, just the after-effects.

Maybe I should start with what I remembered about the house before I cleaned it up?

Maybe there was some clue that I hadn't noticed because I didn't know that I needed clues when I cleaned. I opened the file and wrote panties on the ceiling fan. Or was the bra on the ceiling fan and the panties under the sink?

Man, I was going to suck at this.

Those panties and the bra had to be a clue. Maybe the murderer was a D cup woman who went commando around town.

That didn't help. I suspected there were a lot of women in LA who went commando. I tried to jot down other things I remembered cleaning. I'd steamed footprints, polished the award...

The doorbell rang.

Maybe it was Tiny. She'd ignored my plea for some quiet time and had come over to sit with me.

Aw, what a good friend. It was that friend ESP thing again. Tiny and I had it in spades.

I opened the door, ready to be swept into her hug.

There would be no hugging tonight.

"You," I said by way of a very impolite, less-than-enthusiastic greeting.

You being one Detective Parker. Darn, he still looked hot. Maybe even hotter than he looked at Mr. Banning's. Yeah he was right up there with all my hunky fictional detectives in his hotness. He was Nathan Fillion's *Castle*'s hot. Oh, wait, better yet, he was Nathan Fillion's *Firefly*'s Captain Mal hot. Not that *Firefly* was a detective show that had any bearing on my case.

And not that I cared that Detective Parker was hot.

He was the man who wanted to fry me in the electric chair, if California had one. Maybe that's what I'd do after I finished writing my list...look up whether or not California had the death penalty. Then find out what method they used if they did.

I like to be prepared for any eventuality.

"Ms. Mac. Can I come in?" he asked in his low, gravely voice. It was the kind of voice that made knees go weak. The kind of voice meant for whispering suggestive phrases.

But the man attached to the seductive voice wanted to put me in jail for a crime I didn't commit. I forced my wobbly knees to lock straight and I faced Mr. Sexy Voice.

"I'm sure you can, but that's not what you meant to ask. You meant to ask, *May I come in*. And the answer is, I don't think so." Okay, so that sounded sort of hostile, but hell, I was feeling sort of hostile. This man thought of me as a suspect and not just a hot babe.

Or even a semi-warm babe.

"I really need to ask you some more questions," he said, all businessy sounding. He edged his foot into the space between the door and the frame.

I wondered if he could arrest me for assault if I slammed the door on it?

Thinking about slamming his foot made me smile and I felt a bit better, a bit stronger. "I have a lawyer. He says I'm not to talk to you without him being present."

I also had a file folder. I didn't need super-cop to solve the mystery. I was going to do it myself.

"A lawyer?" he said. "That was fast for someone who's innocent."

"Hey, I know how you cops work. You need to pin this crime on someone before all the other Mortie winners in LA get nervous. And how about all the Emmy and Oscar winners? Golden Globes? Kids' Choice, even? You could have a city in panic. Since I was at Mr. Banning's and accidently cleaned the murder scene, I'd be a handy target. Well, I'm not going to jail for something I didn't do."

"Listen, lady," he said, a hint of frustration in his voice. "I told you, I have to investigate you simply because of the circumstances. But I don't seriously look at you as a suspect. There's no motive."

"How do you know? Maybe I had an affair with Mr. Banning. Maybe it ended badly. Maybe I walked in to find his new babe's undies hanging from the chandelier, her bra under the sink because he had a topless-woman-washing-dishes fetish. Maybe I went nuts and did him in. You don't know. If that's the kind of investigation you run, then I'm doomed."

Oh, geesh, way to go Quincy. Try and convince the cop you did it. I shook my head.

He was shaking his head as well. "Did you have an affair with him?"

"No."

"Did you kill him?"

"No. But you don't know that," I pointed out.

"Ah, but now I do," he grinned, as if he'd won some point. "You just told me. And how about helping me out some more and telling me what I need to know?"

"Like I said, I can't talk to you without my lawyer." I should have slammed the door and taken a chance at assault charges, but curiosity won out. "But what exactly did you want to know?"

"I want you to tell me everything you can remember about what the house looked like before you cleaned it."

Great minds think alike.

I guess I had detective potential after all. I'd been on the right track. Trying to remember what the house had been like … that was a great idea.

And his request sounded innocent enough. Not as if he was looking for a way to convict me, but rather like he was looking for the real killer.

"So, can I come in?" he asked with an endearing little grin that probably made women between the ages of eighteen and eighty not only say *yes*, but say *oh, yes* to anything he asked.

I glanced over my shoulder.

The boys' packing debris littered the living room.

I was tempted to say yes anyway, but didn't want him thinking I was a pig. I was a maid...I should have a clean house.

"Sorry, but no," I said.

"Are you hiding something?"

Sure I was hiding something...a huge mess. But I wasn't about to tell him that. "Unless you have a warrant, you are not coming into my house."

The endearing grin faded away, replaced by a narrowed-eyed look.

Slowly, he said, "I could probably get one."

"How long would it take?" I asked, trying to decide if I'd have time to clean up before he could get back with one.

"Why?" he asked.

I shrugged. "Just because I'm curious."

"Listen, I'm not here to arrest you, I just want some information about the condition Banning's place was in when you arrived."

I didn't say anything. I was glowing with the knowledge that I'd been on the right investigative track and feeling more than a little a bit smug.

At least I felt smug until he said, "Fine, if I can't come in, then let's take this down to the station. You can call that lawyer of yours and have him meet us there. But I'd advise you to cooperate. I might not think you had anything to do with the murder, but I might just start thinking about obstruction charges."

Darn.

I didn't want to go to the station, but I wasn't about to let him in my house.

Thinking fast, I said, "How about a compromise?"

"A compromise?" His eyes were still narrow as he studied me. I was used to the pretty-boy well-waxed eyebrows of Hollywood. Detective Parker was not one of those. As a matter of fact, his eyebrows bordered on bushy, but not in an offensive way, but rather in an I'm-a-real-man-with-a-real-job sort of way. And since right now his job was finding Mr. Banning's killer—a mysterious someone I knew wasn't me—I found his sort of bushy eyebrows comforting.

I realized he was waiting for me to respond as I studied his eyebrows, so I nodded. "Yes. I don't want to let you in, but I don't want to go to the station. So, let's go somewhere else and I'll tell you what I can remember."

"And your lawyer?" he asked slowly.

"I don't think he'd mind my cooperating with your request. After all, I might remember something that will help you find the real killer. And I can't tell you how much I want you to find the real killer."

"Fine. Let's go."

"Hold a minute. Let me get my purse." I shut the door in his face.

I looked at the huge mess.

I was going to come home and clean it, whether or not I felt like it. I was a maid, which meant I had a certain cleanliness standard to uphold. So I'd clean before I started my own investigation into Mr. Banning's murder.

I hurried back out the door, shut and locked it, then turned to the detective.

"Okay, where do you want to go?" I asked. "I'll meet you there."

"Why don't you ride with me?"

"Why do you want me to ride with you? Because you're afraid I'll escape?"

"No," he said, and then in a softer tone he muttered, "You're absolutely driving me insane." His voice rose again as he finished, "I thought you could ride with me because it will simplify things."

Now it was my turn. I sighed one of my big you're-driving-me-nuts-as-well sighs. I normally reserved them for my ex-husband or the boys, but I didn't figure they'd mind me using one on Detective Parker.

"Fine," I said.

I sucked in my stomach and started down the stairs. I stopped at the bottom, gripped the rail hard. I felt sort of light-headed.

He turned. "Are you okay?"

"Fine," I said again, but I lied. I didn't feel fine at all. I felt shaky at best.

Detective Parker gave me a hard look. Not the sort of oh-baby look he probably gave other women. This was an assessing sort of look. He'd given me those before and I recognized it.

But even if it wasn't designed to, that look made my knees feel weak in a way that had nothing to do with my light-headedness.

"When's the last time you ate?" he asked.

I thought about it. It's never a good sign when you have to think about when your last meal was. "This morning."

"Lady, you need a keeper. Come on," he grumbled and took my elbow. It wasn't a police hold, but more of a supportive sort of thing.

He mumbled to himself about ditzy women who cleaned up murder scenes and couldn't even remember to eat.

I should have felt insulted—I am many things, but I am not ditzy—but the day had been too bizarre for me to feel anything but sort of numb.

He tucked me into a very plain looking dark sedan and got in on the other side. I was thankful to find myself in the front seat, not the back, although his car didn't have that plastic police barrier and the back seat looked rather normal from where I was sitting.

I glanced from the normal back seat I wasn't in, to the man driving. "What's your name?" I asked. "I don't like referring to you as Detective Parker. It reminds me that you want to send me up the river. Or is it down the river?"

"I don't want to send you in any direction on any river. To be perfectly honest, I want to finish this interview, clear you, then get as far away from you as I can."

"Yeah, men tend to have that reaction to me." He hadn't told me his name, and I wasn't about to ask again.

I had my pride.

We drove a few minutes in silence.

I jumped when he said, "It's Caleb. You can call me Cal."

"Cal. That's nice," I said.

It was a good solid name. The name of someone you could count on.

"You can call me Quincy," I added.

"I'd planned to."

That was sort of rude, but I didn't comment on his lack of manners. Instead, I asked the question that had been burning away at my brain. "Hey, Cal, do you know if California has the death penalty?"

"What?" he asked. He took his eyes off the road and glanced at me.

"Watch the road," I scolded. I didn't need a traffic accident on top of everything else that had happened today.

"I mean," I said, when he'd turned his attention back to the road, "I just want to know if you convict me for murdering Mr. Banning, am I facing life in prison, or death row? I already know that if I go to jail I'll end up tattooed like Uncle Bill. I'm thinking a unicorn ... a permanent statement of my innocence. But I'm not sure a unicorn tattoo would age well. What do you think?"

"Listen, lady—"

"Quincy. You were going to call me Quincy, remember?"

"You are not going to jail, Quincy. You are not going on death row. And you are not getting a tattoo, unicorn or a skull and cross-bones. You're going for pasta. My buddy makes the best in LA. You look like crap. I'm going to feed you and then you're going to tell me everything you can remember about Banning's place. Then I'm taking you home and hopefully that will be the last you hear from me."

"But about the death penalty?" I pressed.

"Just sit there and be quiet will you?"

"First you want me to talk, then you want me to shut up. You need to make up your mind."

He didn't respond to that. He just made this strangled, growling sound.

"Do men have PMS? If so, I think you've got it. I recognize the symptoms. Short tempered, surly. You have those two nailed."

"Real men don't get PMS, but they do get surly with suspects who won't shut up."

"Ah ha, you just admitted I'm a suspect." Despite the fact he thought I was a suspect, I felt triumphant. I got him. Man, I was going to make a great detective. I'd wrap up

Mr. Banning's murder in a week and clear my name no problem, no death row and no tattoos.

"Yes, I suspect you," he said, pausing a moment before adding, "Suspect you of severe stupidity, and possibly of having some sanity issues, but I do not suspect you of murder."

"See, surly. Very, very surly. And you just called me dumb. I'm not, you know." Even in the dim light, I could see his lips moving, even though he was silent. I think he was praying. That made me feel a bit better.

A guy who talked to God, probably wasn't in favor of the death penalty and maybe that would help my case.

He pulled up in front of *Big G's Italian Restaurant.*

"Big G's?" I asked.

"Yeah. Tony's last name is Garrakowski. That doesn't exactly say Italian food, does it? And Tony's is a bit cliché as far as names go. So he went with Big G's."

"Oh."

Detective Parker—Cal—got out and walked around the car as if he were going to open my door for me, but I didn't wait. I opened the door myself and got out.

He just shook his head and said, "Come on."

He led me into the small, dim restaurant. He didn't wait to be seated, but took me right through the restaurant and into kitchen.

"Hey, Tony," he said to the man at the big stove.

The man turned. He was shorter than Cal, but unlike the detective, he smiled at me. All Cal did was scowl.

Cal introduced me. "This is Quincy. She needs food, and I need your office."

"Help yourself to the office," Tony said. "Although why you'd want to hide away a woman like that, I don't know."

He took my hand and shook it. "Tony. Tony Garrakowski. They call me the Big G. Want to know why?"

It was such an outrageous statement that I couldn't help but smile. "Quincy Mac," I said. "And I don't think you should tell me why...at least not the first time we meet."

To be honest, the Big G wasn't all that big. Maybe five nine, but he had a nice smile and dark black hair that was peppered with the lightest hint of grey. He must be the same age as male-PMSing Detective Cal Parker.

I liked Big G better. He was going to feed me, not send me to death row.

"I'll save it the explanation for the next time then," he promised. "Are you married?"

Cal didn't seem to like Tony's promise to tell me next time, or maybe he didn't like Tony asking if I was married. Either way, Cal scowled, obviously not impressed with my conversation with his buddy.

"No, I'm not married anymore," I said as I smiled at Cal.

"Good to know. When you dump Cal here—women always end up dumping him so that's a given. Maybe it's a cop thing, or maybe he's got bad breath. I don't know which, but you can tell me which when you two are over. Anyway, when you've dumped him, come see me. I'm single, employed and have my own teeth."

You know, when you hit almost forty, those were three qualities a woman wants in a man.

"I use Listerine every day and I'm not a cop," Big G added. "So whichever Cal's problem is, it's not mine."

Cal continued his very coppish scowling.

It made me feel a bit better than I had all day.

"Maybe I'll just do that," I said and I shot Big G my best smile.

I was flirting. At least, I was pretty sure I was flirting. It had been a long time, so I couldn't be sure.

Cal growled that PMSy sort of growl again and I knew I must of been flirting to make him growl.

Suddenly my dead-body-in-the-bedroom sort of day seemed a little brighter.

"Help yourself to the office and I'll bring you some food," Tony said.

Cal took my elbow again and pulled me further back into the kitchen.

"Come on," he said.

"PMS," I said softly.

He must have heard me because he growled again.

For some reason, that made my smile get big enough to make my face feel stretched—stretched in a good way. If you'd asked me earlier, I'd have said not much could make me smile, given the day I'd had. But here I was, grinning from ear to ear.

Maybe Big G was good for me.

Or maybe Cal was.

Cal wasn't smiling. He was tugging me along.

"Fine," I said. "Let's get this over with."

I let him lead me to Tony's office. And despite my brief bout of pleasure a minute before, I felt nervous.

I'd never been grilled by the cops before, but I had a feeling I wasn't going to like it.

Not like it at all.

He sat at the small round table in the corner of the office, and nodded at the other seat, then he dug in his jacket pocket and pulled out a small notebook.

"Start at the beginning and walk me through everything."

"Wait, aren't you going to shine a light in my face? Something nice and bright so I can't see you?"

"I know this is LA, but I'm not some Hollywood actor. I've interviewed hundreds of suspects, and I've never shined a light on any of them. I can't see why I should start with you."

Suspect. He'd called me a suspect.

I felt sick.

"You were going to take me through your day, step-by-step?" he prompted.

"It seemed like a normal day. Well, normal except the boys left yesterday with their father and stepmother, which meant I didn't wake up this morning to the sound of fighting. Their stepmother, Peri, is only a couple years older than my oldest. I'm thinking of adopting her when Jerry divorces her. I always wanted a daughter."

He ignored my comments about Peri and asked, "So, your day started well?"

I took a deep breath and didn't respond, because I probably should have thought it started well, but I'd missed the boys. "I went to work and walked into my partner's bridal bonanza and she told me we had someone—Theresa—call in sick. It was my turn to cover, so I spent my day in the field cleaning. Tiny and I, we take turns filling in when someone's sick," I added by way of explanation.

"And when you got to the victim's house?"

"Mr. Banning's was the last house of the day and the worst. It was a wreck. There were plates and glasses everywhere. Underwear on the ceiling fan. I didn't realize there was a dead body in the bedroom..." Big G walked into the office with two plates heaped high with salads. He blanched in such a way that I knew he'd overheard the dead body mention.

"I didn't kill him," I assured our host.

"I didn't imagine you did." He shot me a toothy smile that showed off his immaculate white teeth. I wondered if, in addition to owning a restaurant, Tony acted, or wanted to act. That's the thing about Hollywood, everyone's in the business, or wants to be.

"Thanks for that. I'm his," I jerked my finger in Cal's direction, "primary suspect."

"She's not," Cal protested.

"Sure I am. You just said you don't shine lights in suspects' eyes, and why would you start with me. That means I'm a suspect, too, just because I'm good at my job and accidently cleaned the murder scene." I sniffed and turned to Big G. "He," I jerked my finger at Cal again, "seems to think I had something to do with Mr. Banning's murder."

"Cal," the Big G said with disgust in his voice.

"I don't think she did it, but I still have to clear her."

"Yeah, I'm a suspect, when all I was doing was trying to make a living to support myself and my three boys. An honest living. My uncle spent two years in prison for a crime he didn't commit. Now, I'm going to follow in his footsteps. And my boys won't have their mom. They'll have my ex's new wife, Peri, but they think of her as more of a sister than a mother. Peri doesn't know how to raise kids. And my ex? Well, other than marrying women who are practically children, he doesn't know much. He loves the boys, but he's a weekend father at best."

"Cal." The Big G's tone was even more disgusted.

"I don't think she did it," Cal protested loudly. "But she cleaned the damn murder scene and I have to deal with that."

The Big G smiled at me. "If he sends you to jail, I'll bring you pasta with a file in it."

"Aw, thanks." I like this man. I tossed him my equally dazzling smile, flashing him my pearly white teeth. It was that smile and those teeth that got me the gig as *Dazzling*

Smile's spokeswoman. I thought it might be a long-term gig. One of those ad campaigns that brings in residuals for a long time.

Three days before the first airing, they found arsenic in the toothpaste. My shot at toothpaste fame and fortune was spit down the sink. So, I was pretty sure the Big G didn't recognize my dazzling smile.

He dazzled a bit as he smiled back, then left the room.

I took a bite of the salad.

"Wow," I managed as I chewed. This wasn't head lettuce cut up in a bowl and slathered with ranch dressing. This had greens, nuts and dried fruit, with some light dressing on it.

Cal forked up his salad and didn't seem overly appreciative as he chewed it, then asked, "What I want you to do is try to remember everything you cleaned, touched or moved at Banning's house."

So, I tried to remember every step. It was easier because I'd started going over all this for myself and my file. I thought about telling him that. After all, he'd made it clear he didn't consider me a serious suspect. But I still wasn't positive I could trust him, so I simply worked at recreating the list, from picking panties off the ceiling fan, to steam cleaning footprints off the carpet. When I mentioned the Mortie, Cal perked up. "What was on it?"

I shrugged as I swallowed another bite of the salad. "No idea. It was sticky and a sort of rusty brown color. It was all over the base of it."

"Blood?"

"I don't think so, though I've never seen dried blood on a Mortie before, much less cleaned it off. I polished the award, and then I put it on the mantle. It was on the couch when I came in," I added.

Cal made a groaning sound and made a call on his cell. "Test the Mortie for trace evidence of blood."

He waited and I ate undisturbed.

I'd moved from my salad to a plate of pasta that Big G brought back. It was just as good. I was trying to decide what all was in the simple red sauce when Cal's phone rang.

He picked it up, listened and said, "Okay." Then he clicked the button and set his phone down.

He turned to me. "It's official. You cleaned the murder weapon."

All I could think of was a wrinkled unicorn tattoo.

CHAPTER THREE

T HE NEXT MORNING, Tiny came over early with donuts. She tried to comfort me over an apple fritter and coffee. "Honey, this is Hollywood. Everyone wants to kill everyone else here. He'll find other suspects."

"But I cleaned the murder weapon and didn't clean it well enough to get rid of all the traces of blood." I knew I should be a bit gagged by the thought of handling a bloody murder weapon, but what got my goat was that I had failed to clean it well enough to remove all the residue. And by residue, I mean blood. I know I should be happy there was some left, so the cops knew it was the murder weapon. That might aid Cal's investigation. But I felt as if I'd somehow been a slacker.

I sighed. "Well, the good news is, Cal doesn't seem to really think I did it. I don't think I'm going to have to investigate on my own in order to clear my name."

"I'm glad," Tiny said.

I glanced at her. There was something about her voice that sounded off. And she looked... well, very un-Tiny-like. "What's wrong?"

"I may need an investigator of my own." Tiny sniffed. And it wasn't the kind of sniffle she had when she thought about marrying Sal. I'd heard those often in the last months when she chose a dress, or the cake. Heck, she'd had one of those watery sniffles when she made an appointment to get our hair done on her wedding day. I wasn't sure scheduling a hair appointment was sniffle-worthy, but Tiny sniffled over every aspect of the wedding.

This wasn't that kind of sniffle.

"Why would you need an investigator?" I asked slowly.

"Well, there's a chance I'm going to end up on the list of suspects." She sniffed again.

"Tiny, Mr. Banning was a client, and if that's their only requirement, then everyone here at Mac'Cleaners will be a suspect. Heck, the fact that Theresa was supposed to clean the house and called in sick would make her a very viable suspect." I thought about my file. I'd have to add Theresa's name, but I really couldn't see our five foot two, size zero employee whacking Mr. Banning over the head with enough force to kill him.

"You said you didn't see any signs of forced entry?" Tiny asked.

I'd thought about this particular question when Cal had asked, after he'd explained I'd cleaned the murder weapon. I'd used the key to open the door when I first arrived and hadn't seen any marks on it. None of the other doors or windows were broken or looked as if they'd been pried open.

I was disappointed that I hadn't thought of it myself, while both Cal, the professional cop, and Tiny, the professional maid, had.

Maybe I wasn't quite as good at this investigating stuff as I thought. It was probably a good thing that Cal didn't suspect me of murder, and I wasn't going to have to clear myself so I didn't get accused of a crime I didn't commit— just inadvertently cleaned up. "No. I didn't see any signs of forced entry."

"Well, the business has a key and I had access to it. I could have gotten into his house without breaking in."

"Yes, but you don't have a motive anymore than I do. Why would you want to kill a client? A paying client?"

I could have understood doing in a deadbeat client like Mr. X—yes, that's how he insisted we refer to him in our files. He's a big industry muckety-muck who was three months behind in paying. He drives a tiny red sports car that screams *I-have-money* and he only eats at the best restaurants—we know because he was famous for telling whoever cleans his house all about it. He'll pay eventually, but we need to be paid on a regular basis in order to pay our own bills.

No, neither of us would kill a man who paid his bill on time.

"Well," Tiny said slowly, then paused for another sniffle, "some might theorize that I might want to get rid of an ex-lover who wasn't happy to find out I was getting married and threatened to show my fiancé some photos."

Dramatic pause.

I knew it was a dramatic pause, not just a sniffle pause, because of Tiny's dramatic expression. Even if you're not an actor in Hollywood, you can't escape learning a bit of drama.

"Photos of *a personal nature*," she explained.

"Oh, Tiny." It seemed like every woman in Hollywood had some photos-of-a-personal-nature floating around town, just waiting to get picked up by one tabloid or another. Maybe that's why I'd never made it big. The most personal-nature photo of me was one of my breastfeeding Miles. And everything was covered in that photo. I don't think any tabloid would be interested in it.

And I realized that thinking about my lack of photos-of-a-personal-nature was easier than thinking about Tiny having them.

"Yeah. Oh," she said. "Being investigated for murder will really put a damper on my wedding." She sniffed dramatically.

My mind sped. What if Cal found out about the pictures? I knew how horrible it was to be considered a suspect. I didn't want that for Tiny. I didn't want my best friend, like my favorite uncle, being sent up or down the river without a paddle for a crime that I knew in my heart of hearts Tiny could never do.

"Don't worry, Tiny. I'm going to find out who did it."

Tiny laughed. "Good one, Quince."

"No, seriously. I planned on clearing my own name. I have a file and everything."

"A file?" she asked.

"Yes. I've started investigating on my own. I'm going to clear both of our names."

"How? I can help."

I shook my head. "No. You've got all you can do to keep the business running and plan your wedding. Let me do this for you."

Tiny sniffed. "Really? You'd do that for me?"

I hugged her. "Hell, if you told me you had indeed murdered someone, I'd offer to help hide the body. That's what best friends do."

"Best friends help you bury the body…and prove you didn't murder someone. There's a t-shirt in that."

We both laughed, because the only alternative was crying, and I didn't want to go there. I had too much to do.

I'd missed something basic like noticing if there was forced entry.

Maybe my file wasn't going to cut it.

I needed to see the big picture. I thought about *The Closer.* It was my favorite cop show, and I really liked cop shows so that was saying something. *The Closer* gang used a big whiteboard where they displayed pictures and timelines so they could study them. Oh, and JD Robb's cop character, Eve Dallas, did the same.

Now, those were two women cops I admired. If a murder board was good enough for them, it was good enough for me.

I left Tiny with assurances that I'd solve this case.

I had a plan ... of sorts.

First thing on my list was a big whiteboard.

Later that morning, I swore as I propped the stupid whiteboard against the bush. I fumbled through my purse for my keys.

Yes, I know I should have simply left them out when I took them out of the ignition. That would have made sense. But the whiteboard was cumbersome and required both my hands to half drag, half carry it from the car to the house, so I'd dropped the keys in my purse without thinking.

Here's two basic truths no one ever tells women.

Number one. When you become a mom, you must start carrying a giant purse in order to haul all the things you, your kids, their friends, their friends' parent, the football team or a random teacher might need.

Number two. Because you carry so much just-in-case paraphernalia, you will never be able to find anything you might want.

As I searched for my keys, I found a small packet of tissues. Feminine hygiene products. A pack of gum. Two packs of mints. An extra pair of nylons, though I rarely, if ever, wore them. A bottle of nail polish.

I also found bandages. Disinfectant. And what looked to be an old cleat. I wasn't sure what sport. That's another thing they don't tell you … different sports require different cleats. Who knew?

"Darn," I swore and kept digging. I know, it wasn't much of a curse word, but I had teenage boys and tried to lead by example, so swearing for me entailed words like *darn, rats* and when I really wanted to go for broke, *boogers.*

A third universal truth occurred to me—car keys sink.

Aha. I snagged them and wondered how a key ring could be so heavy. How many of the keys did I actually need?

I managed to drag the board inside and was about to shut the door and get going on solving Mr. Banning's murder when someone said, "Quincy."

I might have only just met Detective Cal Parker, but I knew his voice. My stomach clenched, not so much in worry that he was here to arrest me, but in a state of panic over the thought he'd found the pictures of Tiny.

"May I come in?" he asked.

Now, despite my best intentions, I'd been so preoccupied with the murder, that I still hadn't cleaned a thing. Solving a murder took precedence over cleaning, in my book.

"No."

"What is going on in there?" He peered around me, as if he'd be able to see for himself.

I pulled the door shut behind me. "Maybe an orgy?"

Now, I'd recently admitted to myself that it had been far too long since I'd had sex at all. The idea of an orgy was absolutely ludicrous. It was meant to make him laugh.

He didn't.

Note to self: quipping with cops might not be a good activity.

"Just stand here on my doorstep and ask me what you want to ask. And really, Detective, you could call and see if your visit is convenient."

"I just wanted to check on you. I was worried."

My eyes narrowed. "I suspect that you weren't worried so much about my well-being as you were worried that your prime witness or suspect—you take your pick—had left town."

"Never mind. This was a mistake."

"Probably," I assured him. Then I thought WWBLJD— What would Brenda Leigh Johnson Do? Yes, she always knew just what to do on *The Closer.* I decided I was going to hunt down my murderer in much the same way that particular TV cop would. After all, she was a strong woman. She was polite—a subject that I frequently harped on to my boys. And her fictional police department had been set here in LA.

The Closer was forever sweet-talking her FBI husband into sharing information.

I didn't have an FBI husband, but I had a cop at my doorstep.

Yeah, I liked *The Closer* and hated when it went off the air. But there's a spin-off. And I liked *Major Crimes,* too. There was another strong female detective.

Beggars could not be choosers. I looked at my potential source of information and said, "To be honest, I forgot to eat today. What if I took you out for a quick breakfast? On me, this time."

I wondered if I could write the breakfast off as a business expense. It seemed to me that keeping the two owners of Mac'Cleaners out of jail was good for business and thus, any costs associated with that endeavor should be counted as a business expense. The IRS might disagree, and annoying them scared me more than annoying Cal so I probably wouldn't risk it.

"Even cops need to eat," I tried. "You can quiz me about the murder scene some more, if you like."

Murder wasn't generally my topic of choice for a meal, but if he asked me questions, maybe he'd let something I could use slip.

"Come on. What do you say?" I tried.

"I'd say you're up to something." He shot me a look that was very reminiscent of the looks my parents used to give me when they said those exact same words.

I was well practiced in the appropriate response. "Who, me?"

He looked over my shoulder and at the small view of the house the partially opened door left. "What's the board for?"

"Come to breakfast with me, and maybe I'll tell you."

Cal sighed again. "Fine. I'll drive."

"And I'll follow in my car." I waited for him to argue that it made sense to drive together.

Cal looked as if he was indeed going to argue, then he simply shrugged and said, "Whatever."

We drove to nearby Pattycake's Pancake House. It was only a few blocks from the house and it was one of the boys' favorite breakfast joints. They'd sit around the table and argue the merit of chocolate chip pancakes against blueberry ones.

I missed my boys.

Pattycake was a twig of a woman who looked like she should be a on some runway modeling lingerie rather than serving up homemade pancakes in an old silver diner car.

We got situated in a booth and placed our orders.

"So, why can't I come in your house?" Cal added a creamer to his coffee.

"You didn't buy the orgy story?" I asked.

"No." He took a sip of his coffee, grimaced and added another creamer.

"What if I said I was hiding escaped convicts in the living room?" I tried.

"Quincy." His voice dripped with exasperation, but maybe, just maybe, underneath that was the slightest sound of humor.

It was that tiny indication of humanity that convinced me to tell the truth. "Fine. So, my boys left for a summer vacation with their father on Thursday, and I've been so wrapped up in this murder business, I haven't had time to clean up."

Cal looked at me like I was nuts—I was beginning to think that was the only expression he had when I was around.

"I'm a guy," he said ... as if I didn't know that. "I wouldn't have noticed."

"You're a detective, which means you make your living noticing stuff. And I make my living cleaning up messes. Having my own home look like a tornado went through it, not once but twice ... that's just embarrassing."

"So what was the whiteboard for?" He took another sip of his coffee and didn't grimace, so I figured he'd added enough creamer.

I wanted to tell him about the whiteboard, and about Tiny. But I couldn't. I may have been honest about the state of my house, but I wasn't willing to give up all my secrets. And I especially wasn't willing to give up Tiny's secrets. "A new craft project," I said, thinking on the fly. "I'm using it to make a huge montage of pictures for my son Hunter. He just graduated from high school and I thought he'd enjoy a sort of Hunter retrospective."

As I said the words, I realized what a stupid explanation that was. Now, if I'd made something like that for Hunter's graduation party in June, it would have made sense, but having it for him before he left for college was dumb.

But obviously, Detective Parker didn't think very highly of my mentality because he nodded and said, "Oh."

HOLLY JACOBS

He'd bought it.

I sort of wanted to kick him because the fact that he'd bought it was insulting. But I needed information about the murder more. "So have you made any progress on finding poor Mr. Banning's murderer?"

Cal looked suspicious. "Why do you ask?"

"Since I'm your prime suspect, it's in my interest to ask if your focus has shifted elsewhere."

"You aren't my focus," he assured me.

"Oh, yeah? So why were you at my doorstep before lunch?"

Now, I hadn't known Cal Parker long, but the low, strangled sound he made as a response didn't take a life-long friendship to interpret. "You aren't my investigation's focus," he managed to say in a tight, forced voice.

"If I'm not your investigation's focus…" A light bulb went off in my head. "Oh." I thought about it some more. "Oh."

"Oh. Oh. What?"

"If I'm not your investigation's focus, then I must be a personal focus." Part of me wanted to holler, *Cal and Quincy sitting in a tree.* It had been a long time since a man was interested in me, but I sensed rubbing in Cal's obvious infatuation wasn't wise. I was a bit curvier than I used to be, but I could say in a very humble way, my mamma didn't have to tie a pork chop around my neck to get the dog to play with me.

"I am not…" Cal sputtered to a halt.

I pushed away the rest of my cinnamon roll, sipped the last of my coffee and stood, careful to suck in my baby pooch. "I think the gentleman doth protest too much," I called out as my parting salvo. I wish I'd learned to sashay better, but since I wasn't much of a sashayer, I sauntered to

48

the door with as much confidence as I could. I ignored the fact I was sucking in my baby pooch for all I was worth. And I ignored the fact that my butt was larger than I'd like and that was Cal's view at the moment.

He hadn't come over to grill me for more information on the case.

He'd come over because he was worried about me.

And he'd never once asked me about Tiny, so odds are he hadn't found pictures of her yet, or if he had, he didn't know she was my partner in the business and had access to a key.

Well, I'd just make sure he didn't meet Tiny. At least, that he didn't meet her until I solved the case. I'd have to distract him.

Now, that would be a hardship, I'm sure.

I chuckled to myself as I got in my car and drove home.

I had a murder board to put together ... and a house to clean.

CHAPTER FOUR

IT HAD BEEN A PRODUCTIVE DAY. I'd found out about Tiny and Banning. I ate a fritter. I had coffee with Cal.

Let's not forget about eating at Big G's the night before. It had been productive and calorie rich.

I was going to start dieting...as soon as I found out who killed Mr. Banning.

And I was on my way to finding that out. The murder board was safely tucked away in Hunter's newly cleaned room. It was a thing of beauty, thanks to my television enhanced investigative skills.

At the top of the murder board was WWBLJD. *What would Brenda Leigh Johnson do*? That was how I was going to solve this case, as if I were *The Closer*.

I wish that show had been around when I was still actively acting. I'd have loved a role on it. I was in a mystery pilot once. Dead Body Number One. That was my name. The pilot never got picked up. Since that and my almost shot at toothpaste fame were the heights of my acting experience, I thought that Mac'Cleaners gave me a better shot of financial stability.

Plus, staying still was not my forte. I haven't played a dead body since. It sounds like it should be easy money, but in fact, it was excruciating.

Thinking about playing a dead body made me remember poor Mr. Banning. Problem was, he wasn't playing. I shuddered.

After I picked up some of the living room and set the board up, I hit the Internet. Thank goodness for sites like *Starkly Wild* and *Hollywood Action*. Plus, I do rudimentary background checks on new clients for Mac'Cleaners. I've had a bit of experience.

I started with a basic Internet search. There were TV shows, films and two plays that Steve Banning had written. He'd received the Mortie for *Dead Certain*, a three-season television comedy about a coroner's office. He'd also been nominated for a slew of awards for *Falling Down the Rabbit Hole* in 2008. He hadn't won any.

Even if he was a dog, I felt bad about that.

I needed more than his professional stats. According to all my television cop shows, every good detective knows that most victims are murdered by someone they know. Frequently, someone they were intimate with. The fact that there was no forced entry indicated that the victim let the killer in, or the killer had a key. Either way, it seemed likely I was looking for someone he knew.

According to the Internet, he had two ex-wives. Tessa Compernalle. He'd been married to her for ten years. After he divorced her, he married Shannon Ball, now Banning. He'd had an affair with Shannon while he was married to Tessa, and they'd had an illegitimate daughter, Shaley. Shaley was nineteen now. Banning had married Shannon when Shaley was five and he'd divorced her as soon as Shaley turned eighteen.

I couldn't decide if that made Banning a nice guy, for staying with his wife for his daughter's sake, or a creep.

I thought about the underwear and the fact he'd had an affair with wife two while he was married to wife one. I wondered when Tiny had her affair with him? Had he still been married to wife number two?

I hadn't asked a lot of questions because I knew Tiny hadn't done it. But given that she'd been with Sal for a few years, it seemed likely. More than likely, he must have been married at the time. She couldn't have known, which meant he'd lied to her, in addition to taking compromising photos.

Let's face it, before Sal, Tiny had horrible luck with men.

Yeah, Mr. Banning was a creep.

I printed out pictures of his exes and daughter and as the printer whirred, I started looking into the newest ex. They'd been divorced almost a year.

According to the Internet, Shannon Banning was going to be hosting a charity gala at Le Celebre Hotel tomorrow. I could get a look at the suspect if I could wrangle an invite.

I did know a few Hollywood sorts—people I'd met while I was married to Jerry—who might attend. But no one well enough to ask for an invite.

But I did know Honey Martin, head chef at Le Celebre Hotel's restaurant, Psst. Oh, we'd also bowled together on a league a few years ago.

That's right. I bowl. I bowl badly, but I bowl.

I knew Honey on two fronts. One being she'd worked with us for a while. She'd been in school and had a daughter. We'd worked her schedule around her classes and family life. Secondly, I knew her because her daughter Trixie was in school with Miles. They would start their senior year together next month.

I felt a bit misty at the thought. Hunter was leaving for college next month, Miles next year and then Eli the year after that. I'd have an empty nest.

Or a jail cell if I didn't figure out who'd killed Banning. I called Honey.

Which is why I ended up in Le Celebre's ballroom on Sunday night wearing black trousers, a white dress shirt and a black bowtie.

I was one of the invisible multitude in Hollywood.

I was a server.

I don't think most people really think about how invisible service people are. I mean, totally look-right-through-them sort of invisible. The upper echelon never sees us, never pay attention. Oh, maybe you note that your waiter did a good job and leave a hefty tip, but when's the last time you noticed a janitor, or the garbage man? When's the last time you said thank you to a postman or the paper guy? Catering staff tended to be of that ilk. You could be served hors d'oeuvres by someone, but if asked ten minutes later, odds are you couldn't describe the person with the tray.

I was counting on that.

I circulated the room, passing out shrimp puffs and listening to bits of conversation.

"…such a shame."

"…what a waste."

My ears perked up as a younger guy—maybe late twenties—talked to a woman who definitely had never sucked in a baby-pooch. "Everyone's boo-hooing, saying all kinds of nice things about him, but let's face it, he's an ass. He had an affair with Shannon while he was still married to his first wife. The tabloids had a field day with it. Then Shannon was shocked last year to find he was having an affair—and had had numerous affairs since. She was even more shocked that he wanted a divorce. He's an ass."

Well, there was someone who called it like he saw it.

I circulated back into the kitchen and found Honey. I pointed through the kitchen pass-through. "What's that guy's name?" I pointed to the he's-an-ass speaker.

"Rogers. I don't know his first name. I think he's here with Shaley. His parents own a chain of upscale boutiques."

"Trust-fund kid?" I asked.

"You can say that again."

I nodded, picked up another tray and made the rounds again.

I spotted Banning's ex, Shannon Ball Banning. I recognized her from the photo I had taped to my whiteboard. She was standing near the bar, talking earnestly to some man I didn't recognize. I sidled up to the bar, tray of shrimp puffs in hand, and listened.

"...Shaley gets it all?" the man asked.

By gets it all, I assumed he meant Banning's estate.

"Unless Steve changed his will again. His dying is the best thing that could have happened to her. Poor Shaley had to leave Yale before the end of term because he forgot to pay the tuition. Forgot my—"

"Tsk tsk tsk," the man said.

Shannon was quiet a moment. "You're right. It's unseemly to speak ill of the dead, even if I was married to him and know there's very few nice things to say about him. What kind of father could use his daughter's education as a bargaining chip to force me to sign the divorce papers?"

"Did I hear..."

I didn't get to hear any more of the very interesting conversation because what was now an all too familiar voice asked, "What are you doing here?"

"Officer," I said as innocently as I could manage as I turned around and found Cal standing behind me wearing a very appropriate black tie suit.

"Detective," he corrected.

I shrugged, as if I didn't care. I wanted to say something snarky, but I couldn't manage to think of anything. All I could do was look at the very trendy suit and the body it hugged and salivate. Detective Cal Parker was gorgeous.

I'd thought so when he was wearing his I'm-a-detective suit when I first met him, and I thought so now as well.

"Again, what brings you here tonight?" he asked, his eyes narrowing.

I extended the shrimp puff tray toward him. "Puff?"

"You are not here as a server." He studied me a moment, shook his head and added more to himself than me, "I'm not buying it."

He didn't take a puff, so I pulled the tray back. "Buy what, Detective?"

"That you're working here."

"Why else would I be here dressed like this?" I asked. "Obviously, I'm a cater waiter."

"You're here to talk to Banning's ex."

"Is she here?" I looked around as innocently as I could manage, then I turned back to him. "Now, isn't that a coincidence."

"Quincy, I'm serious—"

I cut him off and because I was looking at his scowling expression and not his suit-hugged body, I managed to tease, "You're serious? You just informed me you were a detective. Now, I'm confused. Are you serious, or a detective?"

He made a weird sound somewhere between a growl and a cough. "I'm both, and I can arrest you for obstruction, Quincy Mac. Don't push me."

"I think you'd be hard pressed to make that stick. The only conversation I've had with anyone here tonight consists of me asking if they'd like a shrimp puff and them responding. Plus, I'd like to point out that you said to stay in the city ... and this is in the city. I haven't broken any of your rules for potential murder suspects and accidental murder scene cleaner-uppers."

Technically Celebre Hotel was the city, but compared to where I lived and worked, it might as well have been on another planet. Once I attended events like this as Mrs. Jerome Smith, but that was a lifetime ago. It didn't seem real any longer. These days, the only visiting I did on this side of town was clean a house or in this case, serve a party.

"How about me saying to leave this case alone?"

"I haven't done anything to interfere with your case, Detective Serious. So what lead are you following here?" I asked, trying to pretend I didn't know that Banning's ex was tossing this shindig.

"Wow, with acting that impressive, it's surprising you don't have a Mortie."

Ouch.

I decided that this play of wits wasn't fair ... my whole wit was obviously going to beat his halfwit. To be honest, half a wit might be too generous a description of Detective Parker.

I picked up my tray and walked away from him.

"Quincy, I'm sorry," he called.

I turned around. "That's Ms. Mac to you. And although it isn't nearly as glamorous as acting and winning a Mortie, or being a serious detective chasing down a lead, the fact is, I have a job to do, and like I told you when you asked me about cleaning that apartment, I take my work very seriously and I do an excellent job."

I walked away, tray of shrimp puffs offered from one person to the next, then I headed into the kitchen. Honey took one look at me and said, "What on earth is wrong?

Did someone try and grope you? I know how the rich and famous can treat the help."

"It's been so long, I'd consider someone copping a feel a compliment. That's a sad comment, but there it is." That had to be why I'd found Serious Parker attractive…I was desperate. He was probably a troll and I'd simply overlooked it because of my current male drought. "I'm going to go make a couple more rounds."

I took another tray of shrimp puffs and walked back into the crowd. I spotted the detective on the north end of the building—Okay, confession. I have no sense of direction. I know that there's a north, south, east and west, but other than that, I don't have a clue. Here in California, if you see the ocean, it's a safe best that's west or at least westerly, but otherwise, I've got nothing. Cal was standing by the main entrance to the room, so that felt like north to me. Because he was there, I headed toward the pseudo-south side of the room.

I spotted Shaley Banning. I recognized her from pictures, but someone had photoshopped those pics because in real life I had an instant impression of the daughter in *Legally Blonde*. I saw the musical a couple years back and loved it. But even if you never saw the musical, you remember the daughter from the movie? The fact the daughter washed her hair after a perm proved she was the murderer? Well, Shaley's hair looked as if a perm couldn't hurt. It was straight and lifeless.

I passed-puffs my way over to her. "Puff?" I asked as I offered her the platter.

"No."

She was seated at a table all by herself. Her eyes were red-rimmed.

"Are you okay?" I asked.

"Yes," she said softly.

I set the tray down and took the seat next to her. I knew from my research that this girl was only a year older than my Hunter. "Are you sure, honey?"

She sniffled. "My dad used to call me that. *Hold on, honey*, he'd say. He'd finish whatever he was typing, slam his laptop close and rest his elbows on its neon case and say, *okay, I'm listening, honey*. I'm pretty sure he called all women honey, just so he mixed them up—there were a lot of them. But still, it was almost a pet-name."

In a creepy sort of way, I thought, but wisely didn't say out loud. "Used to?"

"He's dead. I'm in mourning. And I'm pretty sure that if my mom hadn't had this party planned, she'd have thrown one to celebrate."

"Not fond of each other?"

Shaley laughed. It was a hard brittle sound of someone much older. "That's an understatement. They're recently divorced."

"I'm sorry."

"Don't be. They never should have married. I think my father married her to keep her from suing for child support. It also got her to sign a pre-nup. I think he did a cost analysis and decided it was cheaper that way."

I must have looked surprised that she was so to-the-point.

"I realize he was a bastard. He cheated on Mom my whole life. He pretty much ignored me. I got into Yale, but only made it through a term. He didn't pay the spring tuition because Mom was giving him grief. So here I am, back in LA, reapplying to less expensive schools. I was so mad at him. And now he's dead."

"You have every right to be angry."

"Maybe. But right now..." She shrugged her shoulders, as if she wasn't sure what else to say.

And I hugged her. I hugged her because she had a lousy mother who'd been so wrapped up in herself that she didn't see how traumatized her daughter was and went through with her party anyway. I hugged her for her dead father, who'd been a less than marvelous father when he was alive. I even added an extra squeeze because when Shaley started to feel better and looked in a mirror, she was going to be horrified by her hair.

"I'm so sorry, sweetie."

"You're the nicest cater-waiter I've ever met."

"No. I'm the first cater-waiter that doesn't really care if I lose my job and let you see that I'm nice. See, Auggie over there?" I pointed to a kid who wasn't much older than she was. "He works these things for Honey because he's paying his way through school and the money's good. He lives in a two bedroom apartment with three other guys, and Honey sends home leftover food because she doesn't think any of them eat well."

"The other guys are struggling students, too?"

"Worse. They're struggling actors."

That made her laugh.

"Everyone has a story, sweetie," I said. "Some just hide it better than others. Maybe your father had a story you don't know about."

She looked thoughtful a moment. "He does—did—have a new girlfriend who seems—seemed—different than some of the other ones. Maybe my dad had a story and wasn't the jerk I thought he was?"

I was pretty sure that Steve Banning was exactly the jerk both Shaley and I thought he was. I felt a stab of sympathy for his new girlfriend, but I didn't say so. If the new girlfriend had discovered he was a big jerk, that might give her motive. But right now I couldn't think about suspects, I had to think about the young woman in front of me.

"Maybe, honey. He was your dad, and no matter what, he loved you in his own way."

She sniffed again. "Thank you. No one else has had one nice thing to say about him."

"I'm glad I could help."

She looked over at Auggie. "Do you think this Honey might consider giving me a job? My mom is more worried about keeping up appearances in order to catch a new husband. She's not going to help me with college costs."

Gossip had it that Shaley was going to inherit whatever money her father had left. I hoped it was enough for her to go back to Yale. But even if it was, working for something is a great life lesson. "I'll put in a good word for you. Honey's back in the kitchen. Why don't you sneak back there and introduce yourself when things out here wind down? Tell her I sent you."

"Thanks." She smiled. "I didn't ask your name."

Of course she hadn't. Until a few minutes ago, I'd been invisible. But she saw me now, and I suspected in the future that she'd see other things clearer as well. "Quincy. Quincy Mac."

"Well, thank you, Quincy Mac."

I picked up the tray of rather cold puffs and started making the rounds again. There's something comforting about being invisible. I pasted on a social smile, asked, "Shrimp puff?" and thought.

Banning had a new girlfriend. Someone who seemed different to Shaley. I'd have do some investigating and find out a name.

"Shrimp puff?"

It would have been easier to ask Shaley the new girlfriend's name, but I couldn't use her.

"Shrimp puff?"

"What was that all about?" Detective Not-So-Friendly jerked his head in Shaley's direction.

I thought I was on the east side of the ballroom. Drat my sense of direction—or rather my lack thereof.

"What was what all about? I'm just passing out shrimp puffs. Either take one, or get out of my way, I need to clear this tray."

He took one and said, "The girl. I saw you talking to, then hugging the girl."

I gave him a mom-look and he shoved the puff in his mouth and reached for another, presumably to keep me talking.

"The poor girl said she's lost her father recently. I was comforting her. That's what moms do. They comfort."

"Don't try a mom-card. You know she's Banning's daughter."

"She is?" I thought back to acting class with Mr. Magee, and tried for my best innocent eye-bat.

"Obstruction," he said in a low, menacing warning. Then he shoved the puff in his mouth.

It's hard to look menacing with a puff in your mouth.

"I have no idea what you're talking about."

He took another puff, but rather than waiting around to hear what else he had to say, I left and circulated with the rest of my tray.

I finished the night off, told Honey about Shaley. Honey's daughter is seventeen and she's mom enough to know how deeply kids can hurt, so she was sympathetic and promised to help.

There's a difference between moms and mothers. Shaley had a mother—someone who was genetically tied to her, but from where I stood, wasn't very emotionally invested. Honey was a mom. She'd do anything for Trixie ... well, except give the poor girl a better nickname. Trixie was really Beatrix. And Honey, being a fan of the Trixie Belden series, and not a fan at all of her mother-in-law from whom her daughter got her name, called her Trixie. Honey and Trixie? I'd read the books and got it.

I'm not sure Honey's ex or his mother ever got it, but they hated Trixie's nickname.

Anyway, Honey was a mom first and foremost. She would take Shaley under her wings.

I thought about Shaley's mother.

Granted she wasn't mommish in the least. And Shaley had said she was using what money she had to keep up appearances and snag a new husband.

Murdering an ex wouldn't help with the appearances, or with the new husband.

I didn't think I'd find the murderer, let alone have him look at me and confess, *Yep, I did it.* I wanted to look at the suspects and get a feel for them.

I didn't think Shaley or her mom had killed Banning. I could always come back and take another look if needs be, but for now, I was going to push ahead with other suspects.

Quincy Mac, PI was still in business.

Only problem was, she didn't have any idea what to try next.

Chapter Five

THAT NIGHT, I PUT an *X* through Shaley and Shannon's pictures. No, I didn't have any proof, but until I found information that changed my mind, I didn't think it was either of them. As a mom, I'd learned to trust my gut. When Miles was five, he said no to a donut one morning and I knew, with absolute certainty, that something was wrong.

I'd taken him to the doctor's office, and he confirmed he had a double ear infection. So for now, I'd trust my gut.

That left Banning's current girlfriend—a girlfriend who Shaley thought was different than the others. I needed to find out who she was and check her out. But more than the new girlfriend, there was the other wife. After all, nothing says murder like a woman scorned. I'd watched enough murder mysteries to know that.

And having been a scorned wife ... Well, there had been times I felt like killing Jerry, but I'd never acted on it.

He was an awful husband.

A questionable human being.

But he was a good father.

Had Tessa Compernalli ever thought about murdering her ex? And had she'd gone beyond thinking and acted? And Banning's new girlfriend? I wasn't sure who she was, but if the panties and bra at his house weren't hers, she might have motive. The file said DOG after all. Again, that woman scorned thing.

The two of them were the next step in my investigation.

I did some Googling and started scribbling in my file. I didn't find any articles that linked Banning to a new woman. I sighed. I didn't want to go back to Shaley for the same reason I didn't press her at the party—she was hurting. But there was another way. I knew who might know who Banning was dating. The question was, how to get Cal to share that information?

I took a piece of paper and drew a circle and wrote *new girlfriend* under it, then posted it on my board next to the pictures of Banning's exes.

So, Tessa, NG and…

Finally, there was Tiny. She wasn't on my suspect list and I refused to put her picture on my board but she'd be on the cops' list if they found out about the pictures Banning had taken. If I couldn't find the real killer, I'd have to check out her alibi. Not that I thought she could do it, but to be ready if Cal found out about the pictures and checked into her.

There was a lot to do.

I needed to focus. Tessa was the best suspect left on my list. I'd start with her, and then I'd find out who the new girlfriend was and see if she did it. Maybe they were her panties, but if not, I'd have to see if I could find out who they did belong to.

Now, the question was, how to get to Tessa?

It was three a.m. when it hit me. I knew how to get to her.

I was getting ready to leave for the office in the morning, anxious to implement my plan when the phone rang. Phone calls before work were rarely good things. "Hello?" I answered with trepidation.

"Hi, Mom."

It was my youngest, Eli and he sounded happy. Relief flooded through my body. "Hi, honey. How's vacation?"

"We're trying to teach Peri to surf. She's worse than you. You're awful." He laughed. That was Eli in a nutshell. He found humor in everything.

"Hey, I resemble that remark," I teased.

"Hunter wanted me to see if you're getting out at all? I'm supposed to be discreet, but we both know that I don't do that well. And yes, that's the word he used—discreet. Are you sure he's related to me? A normal teen would say something more like *do it on the sly*. But be discreet?"

"Your brother may be leaving for college next month, but in reality, he's an old man." To be honest, a more accurate explanation was that my oldest got a full dose of the Mac-genes. They were responsible for my brothers and parents need to excel at everything. It was why they were all doctors. It was why they were all top in their respective fields.

I did not have that gene. I had the black-sheep-gene. One that made you follow your own path, even if it led to your utter destruction. My uncle had it. I had it. I was pretty sure that Eli had it, but I wasn't going to mention it to him. I try not to label my kids.

"You can tell Mr. Nosey-Rosy that I was at a posh party last night, and I might have a date tonight." Now, date was a rather broad term for my plans to grill Cal about his investigation, but it wasn't an out-and-out lie.

"Really?" He sounded shocked. As if the thought of my dating had never really occurred to him.

"Yes, a date. With a man and everything," I threw in for good measure.

That made him laugh.

"Go have fun with your dad and Peri."

"Miles will call tomorrow," he said. The boys did that a lot. Split up the days they called. Oh, sometimes they'd all say hi, but generally one son per day talked to me.

"Tell him not to call too early."

"Yeah, you've got a date. A hot date. You might even be out past nine," Eli said. I could hear the laughter in his voice.

I headed into the office.

The cheery sign greeted me as I walked to the front door. Mac'Cleaners. We had a MacLean tartan ribbon woven around the letters. Yes, my family's original surname was MacLean but when my great-grandfather moved to the United States they lost the 'Lean' part and became Mac. That was fair because from all reports, Donald MacLean was not a lean man. His first name was from his mother's side of the family, the McDonalds. When he moved here, he became Don Mac. Short and to the point, I guess.

People in my family tended to give one child in each generation the benefit of both family names. My mom was Judith Quincy. Hence, my name, Quincy Mac.

I'd complain about my name but really it could be worse. Much worse. My parents decided to honor Dad's Scottish heritage when they named my brothers. Gilliean Mull Mac and Malise Duart Mac. The original Gilliean founded the clan and Malise was his son. And the MacLean family home is Castle Duart on the island of Mull. Gilliean goes by Gil Mac. But poor Malise it was either Mal Mac (awful) or Duart Mac (still not good). He goes by Duart Mac because it was the lesser of two evils. We all call him Art.

Well, unless I'm mad at him, then he's Mal Mac.

He hates that.

Really, of the three of us, I got the best of it. Quincy Mac. And using a variation of my historic last name for the business just made sense. All the cute, play-on-words cleaning names were taken and this one played right into our profession.

I'm not sure why thoughts of the company's name and my own family names were on my mind today. Never mind, I did know. Because it was easier to think about my family's weird names than worrying about murder investigations.

I opened the door and went in.

The light was on in Tiny's office, aka wedding central. For the first time ever, I didn't want to go in and face her. But I wasn't a coward, so I went in.

While all the wedding paraphernalia still was the focal point of her decorating scheme, there was no wedding-mania in her expression. No, there was just an exhausted looking woman sitting at her desk.

"Tiny?"

She looked up.

Tiny had been my best friend since Jerry dumped me and I moved into an apartment next to hers. She helped with the boys. She got me a job at the cleaning service she worked for. She held my hand through the divorce. I'd like to think I'd given her the same kind of support, but truth be told, there was no way I'd ever be able to pay her back for all her kindnesses.

Keeping her off Cal's suspect list would be a start though.

"Hey. How are you holding up?" she asked.

That was Tiny in a nutshell. She looked like crap, but she was worried about me.

"I'm fine. I know this isn't a good time but I'm going to be out of the office a bit more than usual for a few days."

"Is it about the murder?"

I didn't want to answer and involve Tiny any more than she already was. "Listen, I can see you're still upset. Don't be. I'll take care of it."

"But what if Sal finds out and—"

"Sal is going to find out because you're going to tell him. You're going to tell him everything."

"He'll think less of me."

I knew that Sal wouldn't hold her past against her. But I understood her worries. What she should be worried about was the police putting her on their suspect list, but her first thoughts were for Sal because she loved him. She loved him absolutely and completely.

And that's how he loved her in return.

With that kind of love, I knew his concern would be for Tiny, not the pictures. But I could understand her fear.

"Tiny, he loves you," I tried, but she still looked scared to death. "Listen, you told me and I don't think less of you. I think you are brilliant and the best friend anyone could ever have. I adore you. So does Sal. More than that, he loves you heart and soul. He can forgive anything. He'll want to be there for you. You just have to talk to him."

"But..."

"Trust me."

She nodded. "I'll trust you and I'll tell him. He deserves to know the truth."

"You'll cover for me the rest of the week?"

"You know I will. For however long it takes."

"Great. I've got to make a few calls."

My first call was to Tessa Compernalle, and then I was going to call a certain cop with a killer voice and see if we could get together for dinner. I planned on grilling...not the food, but him.

That evening, I was sitting at Big G's, drinking a glass of red wine and dipping some whole wheat Italian bread into a plate of peppered olive oil.

"If he stands you up, I'll have dinner with you." Big G had sat down at my table when I came in.

"Thank you." It was nice to feel wanted.

Big G wiggled his massive eyebrows and grinned as he added, "Cal's a good friend, but he doesn't deserve a woman like you."

"Do you hit on all the women who come in here?" I asked.

"Only the very pretty ones."

I snorted. "Pretty is for teenage girls. I'm a mature woman. The mother of three teenagers. I'm not pretty."

"You're beaut—"

"Tony, you are a very nice man, and a wonderful cook but it's not going to happen," I scolded him with a smile.

"That's okay, I just enjoy flirting. And here comes Cal. I really enjoy flirting with you in front of him. He doesn't seem to like it, and I'm a good enough friend to want to annoy him whenever I can."

I laughed. "You two act like my boys."

"What?" Cal said, scowling at me.

Big G got up. "I'd better go finish off your dinners."

I nodded at the chair and grumpy, growly Cal sat down. "Well?"

"I invited you to dinner to pay you back for feeding me the other day. Big G said he knew what you liked."

That obviously wasn't the response he'd anticipated. His scowl eased up a bit. "You didn't have to do that."

"My Uncle Bill says the only things you have to do in life are die and pay taxes. He was always meticulous about paying his taxes because he didn't want to go back to jail."

Talking about dying reminded me of poor Mr. Banning, bludgeoned by his Mortie. A Mortie I cleaned.

A man who'd taken pictures of my best friend.

I was on a mission.

"So, how was work today?" I asked as innocently as I could manage.

Obviously not innocently enough because Cal glared at me. "Are you still *investigating*? If I were the kind of man who used air quotes, I'd have used them around that word."

"Was that humor?" I asked.

"I don't think that you showing up at that party was funny at all."

Darn. I'd reminded him about the party. "I didn't invite you here to discuss the second job I work in order to support my three sons. I asked you here as a way to repay your kindness. I simply asked about your day because I don't know you well enough to ask about anything else."

He frowned, as if he didn't believe me. Which made me feel a little better about his investigating capabilities because, in fact, he shouldn't trust me.

"How was your day?" he countered.

"I heard from my boys and they're having fun on vacation with their dad and stepmother."

"Jerome and Peri," he said with a nod. "The man has more money than Croesus and a habit of marrying girls. That must make you mad."

"How do you know about Jerome?" I asked slowly.

"I'm a detective, remember? You are not. Stay away from suspects."

"Do you want to give me a list of people I should stay away from? I mean, if you don't, I won't have any idea who I can be around and who I can't."

"Quincy, I don't want to charge you with obstruction, but I will, if only to keep you safe from yourself."

Big G appeared at our table with two plates. "Dinner is served."

"Big G, would you threaten to charge a woman who'd invited you to dinner to say thank you with obstruction?"

"Of course not," the he said.

"I didn't think so." I stood. "Would you mind boxing up my dinner? I'll just take it to go. Have a great supper, Detective."

I stormed after Big G, toward the kitchen. Paid the bill and left a hefty tip, then took my to-go bag and left the restaurant by way of the kitchen door. Cal was sitting on my car. "I don't want to see you get hurt," he said. "Someone killed Banning. What if by some fluke you figured out who it was? I don't think the murderer would be pleased. You could be next."

"It's nice that you're worried." It was a little nice. Annoying but nice. I'd been on my own since Jerry and I divorced. It felt odd to have a man care about me. "But seriously, what are the odds I'd even come close to finding the killer—if I were still investigating, which I'm not."

"Fine. Then could we please have dinner together?" He held his own take out box. "I know someplace we can go."

"Fine."

"First things first. Wait here a minute." He went back into Big G's and came out a few minutes later with a bag.

Then we drove in silence.

I should have been grilling him. I should have been trying to find out if he had any new leads on the case that could help me. And by helping me, help Tiny. I needed to find the murderer so they didn't start looking at Tiny.

But instead of trying to find out if Cal knew anything new, I sat back and allowed him to drive me wherever he intended to drive me.

I thought maybe a park. But instead, we pulled in at the Hollywood Bowl. The very quiet, obviously nothing going on tonight, Hollywood Bowl.

He parked the car and grinned. "I know someone who said he could get us in."

A security guard met us and let us in. The two men exchanged how're-you's and seemed to find a brotherhood in the fact they both had badges.

"Trading on your job for favors." I tsked him. "That's a slippery slope, Officer."

"Detective. And I didn't trade anything for a favor. I'll be keeping my eye out for trouble while we picnic here, so you could say, I was doing The Hollywood Bowl a favor."

I laughed at his logic.

The boys and I had picnicked here before. There were lovely little grassy sections that overlooked the amphitheater. They were first come first serve on a concert night. Tonight we were the only people here, so they were all ours.

"This is nice," I said. It wasn't just nice. It was romantic sitting here on a blanket he'd pulled out of the bag he'd brought from Big G.'s. He pulled out glasses, wine and our to-go boxes.

Definitely romantic.

I was out with a man on a romantic sort of date.

Of course, I was here to pump him for information, but for a moment, I was just going to enjoy myself and forget this wasn't a real date. "I've brought the kids here for concerts in the past, and we've picnicked here, but it was busy and crazy. This isn't that."

It was quiet and peaceful. Yeah, it was definitely romantic.

"Tell me about your family," he said.

I studied him as he took a bite of his pasta from the take-out box. Was he interrogating me?

"What do you want to know that you haven't already found out when you investigated me?"

"Quincy…"

I sighed. "Fine. I'm a black sheep."

"Your family's all doctors except you and an uncle."

"Uncle Bill. But despite the fact they don't understand me, they love me. My oldest son, he's a Mac through and through. My youngest is a march-to-the-beat-of-his-own-drum sort of kid."

"Like his mom?"

I nodded. "Maybe."

"And Miles?"

That gave me a start. "You know my kids' names?"

"I know a lot of facts about you, Quincy. But not the rest. As a detective, I collect facts. When I get enough, I can see the big picture. But that's not what I want with you. I want more than the big picture."

Something in me that I'd tucked away for a long time warmed. He wanted to know more about me. I focused on his last question. "Miles is like his father. He's got an ability to see a ton of small details and piece them together to get a great sense of the whole. He's produced and directed his school's plays and…"

Instead of interrogating Cal, I went on a mother-over-load. It's fun to have someone who wants to listen to how great your kids are.

Dinner was over and we had an empty wine bottle and two take-out containers.

"I should get home. It's a work day tomorrow," I said regretfully.

"For me, too," he said.

"Yeah. I want you at top form. Find the killer, Cal. I don't want to go to jail because I accidently cleaned a murder scene." More than that, I didn't want Tiny being investigated, or worse charged, with a murder I knew she hadn't committed.

"Big G. was going to send you a file in some pasta if you do," he teased.

I might not have known it was teasing before, but it was. I was certain. "And what would you do?"

"I'm an officer of the law. I couldn't help you escape, but I'd visit."

"That's not very comforting."

"I wouldn't turn in Big G." He was teasing again.

"And if I escaped and called you from my South American exile, would you go out with me again?"

He smiled in such a way that I knew the teasing was over. "You could bank on it. And if I weren't investigating a case that you're a witness in, I'd lean over and kiss you right now."

"And if you weren't trying to send me up or down the river, I might let you."

We got up and walked toward the car. Cal's hand reached over and took mine.

It was a little gesture, but I sort of melted.

Now, I really had to find Mr. Banning's killer. Not only to keep me untattooed and to keep Tiny's pictures out of the tabloids. We had to find out who murdered Mr. Banning so that I could kiss Cal Parker.

CHAPTER SIX

THE NEXT MORNING, Tessa Compernalle opened the door moments after I knocked on her posh condo's bright red door.

"Hi, I'm Quincy Mac, from Mac'Cleaners. We spoke on the phone."

Tessa was a beautiful woman. But it was a hard, severe sort of beauty. If I were casting Snow White, she would make a wonderful queen. She didn't smile, but tilted her head slightly, as if she were indeed royalty acknowledging a peasant. Dark hair, red lips, pale skin. The whole nine yards.

Oh, if I were casting a vampire show, she'd be perfect as well.

A vampire queen.

But Tessa was an anomaly in Hollywood. Her only connection to the industry that I could find was through her ex-husband. She was a lawyer by trade. Not even some industry lawyer. No, she did corporate sort of law. That much I'd found online.

"And there's no charge?" she asked.

"No, ma'am. It's part of Mac'Cleaners summer introductory program. We're giving away our hour spruce-up services. Of course, we'd love if you became a regular client, but if you don't, we hope that you're happy with our services and that you recommend us to friends and family. Twenty referrals will earn you another spruce-up."

I handed her our 'official' form. The form I'd made up yesterday. "Here are the terms of the promotion."

She read through it, and then looked up at me. "Fine. I checked and your company is legit. I spoke to Karen Mays. She's used your services and had good things to say about your company."

"Thank you. I'm glad Ms. Mays was happy with our cleaning services."

"I am working from my home office, so the rest of the house is yours."

"I'll get started then. Do you mind if I look around and decide what needs done?"

"Feel free. I normally clean on Saturdays, just dusting and the floor. I do the kitchen as I go."

Tessa's home was … *sleek* was the best word I could think of to describe it. It wasn't a mansion by any stretch, but everything about it screamed I-have-taste-and-money. As well as, I-have-nothing-to-prove. The hardwood floors were polished to the point of almost shining. The furniture was all white. I swear, I'd never let my boys in the house. Boys and white furniture do not go together. Boys and black furniture isn't exactly safe either.

There was a full wall of bookshelves. Bookshelves without a paperback in sight. All the books were old and leather.

I walked from there into a formal dining room. The table was some kind of very dark wood and looked like an antique. It was the kind of table I could picture Napoleon eating at. It was far too ornate for my taste. The chairs' seat-cushions were upholstered in a heavy white fabric that seemed to balance beautifully with the equally heavy, dark wood.

The kitchen was stark. White cupboards. White marble counters. A black and white tiled floor. Black canisters. And a vase of bright, red roses.

It was beautiful … and cemented my Snow White impression even further.

I dusted. Then I went out to the van, got my steam mop and did the floors. But basically I looked for clues.

I don't know what I was expecting to find. There wouldn't be a gun since Mr. Banning had been bludgeoned, and I'd already cleaned the murder weapon.

I didn't find anything out of the ordinary or vaguely suspicious.

When I finished dusting and the floors, I made my way to the bedrooms. One of which Tessa obviously used as a home office. She waved as I walked by and continued with her phone call. I dusted her master bedroom and eavesdropped.

"… I know."

There was a long pause as she listened to whatever the other person was saying.

"You can't imagine who'd kill him? I can't imagine who wouldn't, given the opportunity. You know what I went through with the man all those years. And then to find out he'd had a mistress on the side for more than half our marriage?"

She laughed at whatever the other person said. "No, I'd have never murdered him. That's too quick. I just took him for half of everything he owned. Watching him leave the house with just a suitcase and a box of personal items was a worthy revenge."

Another pause.

"Are you kidding? I tied up any of my own assets. He didn't get a cent of mine."

Her laughter was exactly what I'd have imagined the wicked queen sounding like as she fed Snow White the apple and watched her fall. "Darling, never, ever piss off an attorney. We don't have to kill you. We just leave you wishing you were dead."

I didn't need to do any other digging. I was pretty sure that Tessa Compernalle hadn't killed Mr. Banning. No, she'd simply hit him in his wallet and taken half his assets.

I finished cleaning the house and walked back to the office. Tessa walked out and smiled. "You do nice work."

"Thank you. We pride ourselves in doing a good job. You have our card. Please feel free to call us for any of your housekeeping needs. And if you truly like the work, we hope you'll mention us to your friends."

"I will." She shook my hand and studied me for a moment. "Have we met?"

"I used to be married to Jerome Smith."

She grinned and looked much softer because of it. "I used to be married to Steve Banning. That must be it. I never forget a face, though I've been known to forget a name."

"We cleaned for Mr. Banning until …" I left the sentence hanging. "I'm so sorry for your loss."

"I'm afraid he wasn't much of a loss to anyone. He was a narcissist. And a bit of a pig."

She must have realized how that sounded because she shook her head, and her hard smile slipped a notch and suddenly I saw behind the hard façade. There was a woman there who'd been hurt. Who was still hurting all these years later.

"Sorry," she said. "He wasn't much of a human being, but he didn't deserve to die like that. Sometimes, I remember how he was before he made it big in Hollywood. Winning that Mortie was the worst thing that ever happened to him. He spent the rest of his career trying to garner more accolades. Nominations didn't count. He worried more about potential awards than a good product. But I still remember the man who wanted to tell a good story. A man who loved me. That's the man I mourn."

Tessa had to be about my age, but I still felt a maternal need to comfort her. "I'm so sorry."

She gave herself a little shake and then smiled. "Thank you. And thank you for cleaning. It looks wonderful. I will be calling your service again."

I left and was loading up the cleaning van when a car pulled up behind me. Someone got out. The sun was behind them, so it was hard to make out the details. But as the person walked toward me, I heard them growl and I knew who it was. "Officer," I said out of some need to annoy him.

"Detective," He said automatically. "What are you doing here? I warned you about interfering with my investigation."

"I have no idea what you're talking about. I was here cleaning a house. I'm a maid. It's what I do."

He made that loud, low sound of strangled frustration again. "Quincy."

"It's an honest living," I said. "Maybe not glamorous by Hollywood standards, but it's honest, and I'm good at bringing order to chaos." And as I said the words, I realized that's what this investigation was. Taking snippets and bits from Mr. Banning's life and finding some order in them. Heck, I'd been training to be an investigator for my entire adult life.

My epiphany didn't seem to have impressed Cal, nor did my excuse. He just gave me his stern detective look and said, "Quincy," again. Just my name. It was a warning.

"I don't know what you're talking about, but you should know, Tessa didn't do it."

I beat a hasty retreat and left Cal to discover that for himself.

The only problem with crossing suspects off my white-board was that I had fewer and fewer potential murderers to investigate.

CHAPTER SEVEN

NOW THAT I WAS FAIRLY certain Tessa didn't kill Mr. Banning, I wasn't sure what to do next.

I thought about going home, but I knew if I did, I'd stare at my stupid whiteboard. What would the cops on *The Closer* do? Or the new spin-off, *Major Crimes*? (Confession: I loved Mary McDonnell in *Battlestar Galactica*. I have three boys who love science fiction, so I watched the whole series and she'll always be the President to me. Bet Detective Parker didn't find that fact as he investigated me.)

Anyway, I didn't know who the girlfriend was and the only new thing to add to my whiteboard was another X through a suspect's picture. I didn't have a clue what to do next.

Frankly, I didn't have a clue what *CSI* or *Law and Order* would do either.

I drove past a small bar. The Bit Part Bar. I decided I wasn't going back to the office or home.

It wasn't much of a solution, but it was better than staring at a whiteboard for hours.

I went around the block and pulled into the parking lot. The bar wasn't exactly seedy, it was simply under-loved. I don't think anyone had done anything to update it or even clean it thoroughly in years. Maybe whoever named it should have gone with The A List Bar. It was as if calling itself Bit

Part was dooming itself to mediocrity. It was definitely not a bar frequented by Hollywood's beautiful people.

Good thing I wasn't that. I found a seat at the bar and waited to order.

There were some basic truths about the Mac family. Except for my Uncle Bill and me, the Macs were all overachieving doctors. The Macs were beautiful people. My mom had three kids and was still wore a size eight. . . . and sometimes size eight was baggy.

And another quality of the Mac family, Macs were Guinness drinkers. Even my Uncle Bill and me. I glanced at the tap and saw the one I was looking for.

The bartender was working on a computer at the far end of the bar. He glanced at me, sighed and shut the laptop's neon orange case with more force than necessary. He slid it onto a shelf and ambled down to me.

"Guinness, please," I told the bartender.

He was a tall man. Not an overly good-looking man. If I were a casting director, I'd cast him as the best friend, or even better yet, a villain. And if I were here in my housecleaning capacity, I'd encourage him to hire Mac'Cleaners to come give the bar a complete cleaning. He was as mediocre as his bar.

The bartender was silent and stared at me a bit too long to be comfortable. It felt intrusive. Ominous even.

"Is there a problem?" I asked.

He smiled and he didn't look nearly as ominous. He was back to a best friend. That's what I'd cast him as in my imaginary movie.

"Sorry." He smiled broadly now. "You're new here."

"I was driving by and . . ." I shrugged. I didn't know how to explain the fact that I was sitting in a bar in the afternoon. That was definitely out of character.

"Yeah, we don't get many lookers like you," he said again with a grin.

I couldn't help but smile. "Thank you. That's a lovely compliment."

"Willy," he said. "My name's Willy."

Politeness would require me to respond, to tell Willy my name, too. But despite the fact he'd paid me a compliment, I wasn't sure I wanted to, so I simply smiled.

Willy brought me my Guinness a couple minutes later, and then went back to his computer. Its garish case was almost blinding, so I stared at a mural on the wall as I sipped my drink. It was a red carpet scene with a lot of recognizable Hollywood stars. A List stars. A List Bar would really have been a better name.

I stared at my drink. The Guinness made me think about my family.

My mother was a lady. If white gloves came back into fashion, I could easily see her getting a pair. She listened to classical music. She read literary fiction if she read fiction at all. Mainly she read medical tomes.

My mom and I had very little in common.

But my mom loved Guinness. For my twenty-first birthday, she'd come into town I'd left Hunter with Jerry and gone out with my mom. We hadn't stopped at a neighborhood bar. No, my mom was not a neighborhood bar sort of person. We'd gone to an upscale bar on Hollywood Boulevard. But sitting here in The Bit Part Bar with a sheen of dust on its light fixtures, I couldn't help but think of her.

I missed her. We tended to drive each other nuts if we were in the same room for too long, but I did love her and right now, I wished she were here.

"Quincy." I turned. Detective Cal Parker obviously had some sort of tracking system on me because everywhere I went, he turned up.

I sighed. I'd forgotten about Mr. Banning. I'd forgotten about how many times I'd disappointed my mother, and simply been reveling in a memory of one night where we'd simply had fun together.

Now here was Cal to bring me back to the unpleasant realization that I still hadn't found out who'd killed Mr. Banning. Not only had I cleaned his murder scene— accidentally—but my best friend had been blackmailed by the rat.

"I was at Tessa Compernalle's and she said she'd *won* a spruce-up from a certain cleaning service. I thought I'd warned you to stay out of my investigation?" He pulled up the barstool next to mine.

"I don't know what you're talking about," I said as I took a sip of my beer. Maybe Cal didn't have some tracker on me. Maybe I was simply that good. I mean, I seemed to be a step ahead of him in this investigation. The thought made me smile.

He wasn't smiling. He was staring at my drink. "Guinness?"

"With a last name like Mac, would you expect me to drink anything else?"

"Is Mac short for something?"

There was something in his eye that made me say, "You already know, right?"

"I am a detective, and you did clean my murder scene." It wasn't really an answer, but I knew he knew my family's original last name.

The bartender left his computer and came toward us. Cal pointed at my Guinness and nodded.

Willy gave him a long hard stare-down. "You're a cop, aren't you?"

"Yes. Detective Parker."

"Yeah, I saw you on the news. You're investigating that guy who died."

"The guy who was murdered," Cal corrected. "Yes."

"I'll get your Guinness."

"Now about your last name. MacLean," he said. "Mac'Cleaners. Cute."

"Thanks." I remembered how Tiny and I had gone round and round, trying to find a name for our new business. Mac'Cleaners won out. Tiny's TurboClean didn't have the same ring.

"Don't think I forgot you're still investigating the murder," he said conversationally. "You're impeding my investigation and it's got to stop, Quincy."

"I didn't impede anything. I cleaned a house. You can't stop me from making a living," I said just as conversationally. "Go ahead and ask Tessa if I grilled her. She'll tell you I didn't. I cleaned. That's my job."

He stared at me. It was the kind of look I vaguely remembered from my pre-kid days. The kind of look where a man is mentally undressing you. It could be creepy when the wrong man did it, but Cal was the kind of man I wouldn't mind undressing me in real life—well, if he wasn't trying to put me away for murder.

I don't know what he saw as he mentally undressed me, but he smiled, a slow, seductive kind of smile that had probably made women drop their guard or their drawers, depending on the circumstances.

"Do you give all the men in your life this much trouble?" he asked, his voice a low, gravelly sound that probably hastened the dropping of guards or panties in the past.

I couldn't afford to drop either with this man. And since I wasn't immune to his come-hither looks or voice, and didn't feel like throwing cold water on myself, I did the next best thing. I pictured Cal and I in an intimate embrace, then pictured my boys walking in. That mental image was better than cold water.

I almost felt giddy with my well-squelched attraction. "I have three sons, Cal. I give them far more trouble than I've been able to give you, I swear. And I have an ex-husband. I give him more trouble than you and the boys combined. And I sometimes do it just for the fun of it."

He looked slightly confused by my unswoonish reply. As if he couldn't understand how his personal charisma had left me unaffected. I wasn't about to tell him that having three boys was Kryptonite to lust.

"Heaven help your ex," he muttered.

"Someone should help him. That man has a penchant for young girls. Nothing illegal," I hastened to add. I didn't want to see Cal arresting Jerry. Like I said, Jerry's a pig, but he's a good dad. "But younger than a man his age should like. Once they're approaching their mid-twenties, he's done with them. I'm thinking of adopting his current wife. She's only two years older than my oldest and really is the sweetest girl."

Cal gave me an odd look. "You like your husband's current wife?"

"I've liked all my ex-husband's wives, both the current one and those that came before me and after me. He's got good taste in women. He married me, after all, didn't he?"

Cal laughed. "So, does he have kids with all those other wives?"

"No. My boys are his only kids. I don't think he intended to have three kids in three years with me, but it turns out,

86

I'm a fertile Myrtle. Seriously, when it became apparent we were going to separate, I didn't even want to be in the same room with him. I was terrified he'd sneeze, and I'd be pregnant with baby number four."

Cal took another long, slow sip of his beer, then asked, "Was that a warning?"

To which I gave the eloquent response, "Huh?"

"Were you cautioning me that you're fertile so that when we get together, I know we have to be careful?"

I sputtered Guinness all over the bar. And inhaled a bit of it which caused me to literally choke. When I could breathe, I managed, "You are not only the most arrogant man in the universe, you're … deluded. You and I are never going to find ourselves in any sort of position that would require us to be careful. Plus, I'm thirty-eight and my eggs are old now. They're tired. They're fried. Yes, I've got fried eggs, so I'm sure fertility isn't as much an issue now that I'm in my late thirties, as it was when I was in my teens and early twenties."

My response was obviously not what Cal expected. Mr. Come-hither-charcoal-grey eyes looked confused. "I thought you brought it up because you've been thinking about me like that."

"Detective, you can be sure, I've thought about you a lot since I cleaned Mr. Banning's place. But in terms of us getting together like that?" I shook my head. "Not in your dreams. You're trying to arrest me. You're trying to put me in jail and I still haven't looked up if California is a death penalty state, so maybe you're even try to kill me. No matter what, let's be clear I don't sleep with men who want to put me in handcuffs."

"Duly noted as well." He took a long sip of his beer, and then added, "Quincy Mac is not into kink."

"I didn't say that," I assured him.

"Oh, so you're saying that you are into kink? I mean, I know a lot of women like cops because of the uniform, or the handcuffs."

What the heck? I'd put him in his place and assured him in no uncertain terms his normal tactics were not going to work on me. He couldn't charm me into submission. I didn't have a thing for men in uniforms. "You don't have a unif—"

He cut me off. "I have one, I simply don't wear it to work anymore. But if that's your kink thing, I can wear it for you."

I drained the rest of my Guinness because no one in the Mac family wasted Guinness. Then I stood. "There are many things in the world that are uncertain. Right now, the biggest uncertainty for me is, who killed Mr. Banning. But there is one absolute certainty you can bank on. You and I, kink or not. Are. Never. Going. To. Happen."

I walked out then because sometimes saying less is more.

And because imagining Cal in his uniform was a picture that no amount of thinking about kids, or even my parents, could erase.

My living room was respectable looking, but I'd simply shoveled all the boys' things into their rooms. I thought about tackling them.

But I couldn't find the energy.

I called Tiny instead. "Wanna chick-flick it tonight?"

"I'll bring the ice cream."

Half an hour later, Tiny walked in the door. "You really should start locking the door. You just cleaned a murder scene. Door locking needs to be a priority."

"I knew you were coming."

"I'd have waited for you to unlock it." She stopped scolding and held a bag aloft. "Hollywood Walk of Shame Ice Cream. I got a whole gallon."

"Do we need bowls, or just two spoons?"

"Spoons.

The Hollywood Walk of Shame Ice cream was my favorite ice cream, a concoction that no dieting Diva would ever consider. Since I wasn't a Diva, I didn't worry about it and simply dug into the gooey confection. Chocolate jimmies, chocolate chips, brownies, chocolate-covered nuts, chocolate-covered raisins…Well, you get the picture. If it was chocolate, it was probably in it.

I turned on *Legally Blonde*.

It had been on my mind since I met Shaley Banning. It was a chick-flick, but it was also a murder mystery. Elle needed to find out if Brooke Taylor Windham really killed her husband, and if not, who did.

I liked the parallel between Elle Wood's journey and mine. Elle had to keep a sorority sister out of jail…I had to keep my best friend and myself out of jail. Thoughts of my uncle, wrinkled unicorn tattoos and bloodied Mortie's kept flitting through my head.

Who killed Mr. Banning?

I didn't think it was his daughter (spoiler alert) like in *Legally Blonde.*

I didn't think it was either of his ex-wives.

"I need to go see his current girlfriend," I murmured to myself.

Tiny hit pause and stared at me. "Mr. Banning's?"

I nodded.

"Did you find—"

I cut her off. "No, don't ask anything, and don't tell me anything more about your relationship with him. I don't think it's wise for you to talk about it with anyone. Not even me. No one can be called to testify about things they don't know."

"Do you think it will come to that?" she asked, her voice shaky.

"No. I don't. But we have to be smart and plan for every contingency."

She nodded. "But can't you get in to see Cassandra the same way you saw his ex?"

Cassandra? "Wait, you know who Mr. Banning's girlfriend is?"

"Anyone who reads any tabloid knows he's seeing Cassandra Yu." She paused, looked at me and said, "That's right, you don't read industry news."

"I don't mind industry news, I just don't like gossip."

When Jerry and I divorced, there had been gossip. I wasn't a name, but Jerry was well known in the industry. That was enough to make our divorce and his rapid remarriage an item. I'd avoided the gossip mags ever since.

"Cassandra Yu. I'll make a call and tell Cassandra that she's won a free cleaning." I wondered if Cal knew Mr. Banning's girlfriend's name. Probably. He was a cop.

"Now, tell me about the wedding," I said, wanting to change the subject.

Tiny started to talk. All her excitement was back. I'd been worried about her. Nothing should dim her happiness about marrying Sal.

I listened to talk of flower arrangements and bands, reception halls and pictures. Tiny had been driving me crazy for weeks with her plans, but today, listening to my friend was soothing. Things would work out. I'd find out who killed Mr. Banning. I'd find those pictures. And I would wear whatever flouncy, pastel colored dress as I stood up for my best friend at her wedding.

❧ ❧ ❧

Cassandra Yu only lived a couple blocks away from Tessa. She was thrilled that she won Mac'Cleaners spruce-up services, at least that's what she said when I called first thing Thursday morning and made arrangements to come by that afternoon.

However, she didn't look like a happy winner when I showed up.

"It's the first good news I've had in a week," she said as she opened the door and let me in.

Cassandra Yu looked awful. Her eyes were red-rimmed, her face was splotchy. Her dark hair looked as if it might spring to life and start hissing at me in a Medusa head-of-snakes sort of way. She was wearing a pair of sweatpants that were sizes too big and a ratty flannel shirt over a stained t-shirt.

"Please come in," she said.

Her house was neat as a pin other than the couch. It was piled with quilts and pillows. There was a tissue box and waste can next to it.

"Are you okay?" I asked.

"It's been a tough week." She sniffed. "I lost someone— someone I loved. He loved me, too. We were talking about getting married." She shook her head. "Sorry. That's more than you needed to know."

"I'm so sorry for your loss."

"Thank you." She looked at my cleaning kit. "What can I do to help?"

"Nothing. Why don't you just relax? Your house is so neat, this won't take me any time at all."

She nodded and went back to the cocoon she'd built herself on the couch.

I was right, her house wasn't just neat as a pin, it was obvious that she cleaned it thoroughly on a regular basis. I felt bad for her, so I threw in a few extra services like cleaning the windows of her small bungalow.

I hate cleaning windows.

When I'd finished, I asked, "Could I make something? Tea? A sandwich?"

"You don't have to—"

"I'm a mom. This is what I do," I joked, hoping she'd relax and let me do something for her. I didn't have to really talk to her to know that she wasn't the one who'd killed Mr. Banning. She loved him. She was going to marry him— at least she thought they were going to marry. Whether or not they were didn't matter. Whether he was the slimeball I'd thought he was, or he was becoming a better man because of Cassandra didn't matter. She was in pain. She was broken up because of his death.

And suddenly I didn't see Mr. Banning as a dead client, or a blackmailer, or a louse of a father, or a cheating husband.

I saw him through Cassandra's eyes, and he was someone who had been loved.

I guess that was enough of an epitaph for anyone.

"Please, let me do something." I wanted to do something to soothe her.

She shot me a weak smile. "You just cleaned my house."

"Something more than that," I insisted.

"A cup of tea would be nice."

I went to her kitchen and made myself at home, making us both a cup. "I know it's cheeky, but even though we don't know each other, I think you could use someone to talk to. Tell me about the man you love."

"Loved," she said sadly. "He's gone and…" She hiccupped and took a sip of her tea. "Steve wasn't a saint. Don't think I don't know that about him. He was imperfect. He'd made some horrible decisions in the past and done things that hurt other people. But I loved him. And he loved me."

"Knowing he wasn't perfect and loving him despite it, or because of it, well, that says something. What did Steve ... was it?" She nodded and sniffled. "What did Steve do?"

"He was a writer. He won a Mortie, you know."

I did know, but I didn't want her to know I knew. "He must have been good."

"He was. He'd had a bit of a rough patch. He'd been looking for some inspiration. He'd found it at a local bar. He wrote this marvelous script. *Hanky Panky*. He said it was *Cheers* meets *Arsenic and Old Lace*."

"It sounds wonderful," I said.

"It was. He was convinced someone would snap it up, and then he'd have a second Mortie."

"I'm sure he would have."

She took a small sip of her tea. Her eyes got all glassy and she murmured, "I loved watching him work through his process. He'd leave every day and head to this bar, he said it was his muse. Most women wouldn't like that, but he didn't drink anything stronger than coffee. He'd take his gaudy laptop and sit at a booth and write all day. He tipped well, so no one at the bar minded. He said the bartender was his inspiration for the main character." She took another sip and her eyes were shining with unshed tears. "I guess the guy's a real piece of work. He hits on every woman who walks in the dive and doesn't score with any of them."

She cried again. "Like I said, Steve wasn't perfect. He was talented as all get out, and he was perfect for me. He told me his two other marriages were just warm up for me. That was enough."

"That was all the perfect he needed," I assured her.

"I saw him the night he died. We'd had a few friends over, and after they left I washed the dishes." She smiled, despite her tears, and I knew exactly who the underwear belonged to.

Cassandra hadn't killed him in a fit of jealousy. She'd left her underwear at the house of the man she loved.

I looked at this woman who was mourning Mr. Banning's death.

I wanted to find out who murdered him for my own sake and for Tiny's. And suddenly, I wanted to find out who murdered Mr. Banning for Cassandra, too.

Steve Banning wasn't perfect. But he was perfect for Cassandra Yu.

That was a better legacy than any Mortie.

I headed home—another person crossed off my murder list.

I was getting good at eliminating suspects, but nearly as good at figuring out who did it.

I pulled in my driveway.

Another car came right in behind me, blocking me in.

"Hello, Detective. It's so nice to see you. Can I help you with something?"

"You can. You can help me by staying away from my investigation. I keep asking you to. You're not obliging." He stepped right up to me. "What were you doing at Cassandra Yu's house?"

Seriously, tomorrow I was checking my car for some kind of tracking device. The man had an uncanny ability to find out where I'd been.

"Wow, that wasn't a very nice greeting." I stepped around him and headed onto the porch and put my key in the lock. "Try something like, *Why Quincy, don't you look ravishing today in your black slacks and white blouse. I think modern maid outfits are quite as sexy as the old-fashioned French maid ones.*"

He glared, so I added an "Oo la la," for good measure, then I walked into the house and for a moment thought about closing the door on Cal. It would make him nuts, which would be very satisfying. But probably not wise.

There was a saying about don't poke the bear.

A vein throbbed in his forehead in such a way that I didn't think annoying him any more than he already was would be wise.

"Come in if you like."

"You cleaned?" he asked from the doorway, as if nervous about stepping over the threshold.

"A bit. I've been too busy to do a proper job of it, but I'll get to it." *After I find out who killed Mr. Banning.*

He took the step and entered my house. "So, what were you doing at Cassandra Yu's?" he asked as he looked around.

"Would you believe she won a free cleaning, too?" I tried. I headed into the living room, trusting he'd follow.

He did. "No."

"Well, you'd be wrong. She did win a free spruce-up service from Mac'Cleaner's. It's a great promotion for drumming up new business."

"And can you tell me how her name got in the drawing for this marvelous prize?" He took a seat on the couch, not waiting for me to invite him to do so. That was sort of rude.

I gave him my best mom glare and then answered as primly as I possibly could, "I couldn't say."

I remained standing.

He must have figured out I wasn't going to sit down because he stood back up and asked in a low, dangerous sounding voice, "Can you tell me how many entries you had in this amazing promotional drawing of yours?"

"I'm sure I couldn't." I couldn't mainly because telling him only one would annoy him. That vein was bulging and pulsing so fiercely I was afraid the man was going to have a heart attack.

"I know CPR," I said out loud.

"Okay, why does that have anything to do with anything?" The vein stopped throbbing and he went back to looking at me like I was nuts.

That was better than looking at me like he was considering arresting me for obstruction.

"I love the word apoplexy. It's sort of nondescript. A stroke. A heart attack. Something that makes you pass out. Well, you look apoplectic. I told you I knew CPR in an effort to be nice and assure you that if you go down, I'll do my best to revive you." He looked somewhere between apoplectic and annoyed. "Can I get you something to drink?" I threw in for good measure.

"You can get me some answers." Slowly, as if speaking to a not very bright child, he said, "What. Were. You. Doing. At. Cassandra. Yu's. House?"

"Cleaning. It. I'm. A. Maid. A. Good. One." I answered using the same cadence that he'd used.

His face flushed. The vein pulsed.

I flexed my wrists, warming them up for my upcoming test of CPR.

He took a step toward me.

Maybe he wanted me to catch him.

He took another step.

I braced myself.

He reached out for me, probably to lean on me as he collapsed in his apoplectic fit.

I reached out to catch him.

Rather than fall on me, he pulled me into his arms and kissed me.

On. The. Lips.

I leaned into him and wrapped my arms around him. I was ready to whisper *oh-yes*, when he whispered, "You're driving me nuts."

Now, it might have been a long time since I stood in the middle of my living room kissing a man, but I knew that there were much better endearments he could have whispered. My first impulse was to kick him in the shins, but since I preach nonviolence to the boys whose first impulse seems to be pummeling each other on a regular basis, I didn't.

It was a near thing.

Instead, I unwrapped my arms, and pushed against his … rock hard chest.

It was like pushing against a brick wall, if the brick wall in question was all warm and solid and made your knees go a bit mushy.

"What was that for?" he asked.

"Figure it out."

Just then my doorbell rang. I was thankful for the distraction. Because if Cal had figured out a better endearment, there was every reason to think I'd have disregarded the fact he was investigating me for murder and taken him up to my room—which unlike the boys' rooms was clean—and say oh-yes, then have my way with him.

The doorbell was like a mini glass of water in the face. It reminded me that I definitely should not take Cal up to my room.

I opened the door and found my mother.

She wasn't just a mini glass of cold water.

She was a tsunami.

CHAPTER EIGHT

"**M**OTHER," I MANAGED TO spit out. "What are you doing here?"

She breezed into my house and kissed my cheek as if her dropping in unannounced was an every day occurrence.

It wasn't.

"I came to see you, of course. Your father will be along in a moment. He's parking the car, since the other spot in the drive is taken." She looked at me and I knew she was asking who had the audacity to park in the spot she wanted.

Before I could say anything, Cal came into the foyer and said, "Ma'am, Detective Caleb Parker."

"Doctor Judith Quincy Mac." My mother offered her hand in a regal-queen-offering-a-hand-to-a-peasant sort of way. "And you know our Quincy how?"

I waited for him to tell my mother that he'd met me at a crime scene. That he was investigating me as a murder suspect. That he was here to threaten and arrest me for obstruction of justice.

He didn't tell my mother any of that. He said, "We're seeing each other."

I choked.

He laughed. "Quincy's still getting used to the idea. We'd just shared our first kiss when the doorbell rang."

Choking. Trying to catch my breath. I couldn't manage it. There was no air left in the room as my mother and Cal stared at each other. I clawed at my throat, but I still couldn't breathe.

"Quincy," my mother said sharply, scolding me with just my name.

I couldn't decide if she was scolding me for being crass about my death throes, or if she was scolding me because Cal said we were kissing.

Either way, her tone snapped me out of my oxygenless state. I drew a deep breath and informed her, "I am not seeing him in any way other than my eyes register his presence. We are not dating, and that kiss he referred to wasn't a kiss at all. He was apoplectic. I was trying to catch him and help him to the floor in order to perform CPR. I thought I'd finally be able to use the training you forced on me."

My mother shook her head and her perfectly coiffed grey-streaked hair didn't move an inch. "Quincy, you are no longer a teenager who has to hide her dalliances from her parents. You're a grown woman, and you have needs. I understand that. I'm just happy you're satisfying them with a respectable man. Law enforcement is a noble career."

"Hear that, Quincy?" Cal asked with an annoyingly huge smile. "I'm noble."

"You're a pain in my as—"

"Quincy, there is no need for vulgar language, young lady."

My mother had scolded me, called me vulgar and talked about my needs and satisfying them all within minutes of coming into the house.

We hadn't moved beyond the foyer.

Here's the thing. I'm thirty-eight. I'm a business owner. I'm the single mother of three teenaged boys. I am a confident, capable woman.

And minutes after my mother walks into a house, I revert to an unsure, teenaged basket case.

There was a light rap on the door and my father walked in. "Quincy, light of my life."

I ran over and hugged my dad. He whispered in my ear, "How are you, sunshine?"

"Good, Dad. Very good."

He nodded as he released me. Then he spotted Cal. "And this is?"

"Dad, this is Detective Caleb Parker. Cal, this is my father, Dr. Martin Mac." And before Cal could say anything outrageous, I added, "Cal and I aren't dating, and we weren't kissing. He's been filling Mother's head with lies. I think you should have a look at him. He was apoplectic. I thought he was going to pass out so I was trying to give him CPR when his heart or brain or whatever exploded. His lips just fell on mine as he fell."

I had officially used the word apoplectic more than any regency novel ever had, but that last sentence was beyond redundant. I knew it. And I could see that my mother had realized it, too. I waited for her to point it out.

She ignored the redundancy and instead said, "Quincy, apoplectic is not a medical condition."

"I am not a medical practitioner, so I can use whatever term I want." Truth is, I loved the word. I'm not sure what book I read it in when I was just a kid, but it stuck. I didn't get a chance to use it often, so when I could trot it out I did.

My mother hated the word as much as I loved it.

That about summed up my relationship with my mother. Polar opposites.

"Sir, we are dating," Cal said all properly and coppishly respectful. "We've been out to dinner. That's a date, if ever I heard of one. And now, I've met her parents. Our relationship is moving fast." He shot them a charming smile.

I gave in to my baser instincts. I kicked him. I told myself the boys weren't here, so they'd never know. Parents should be allowed to have some secrets from their kids.

"Quincy," my mother reprimanded.

Cal grinned. "Since you both are visiting would you consider letting me take you all to dinner tonight? My friend has a restaurant with some of the best food in the world." Before I could protest he added, "I could call him and ask him to make us my favorite. Gnocchi and cheese. It's like macaroni and cheese, only better. I'm pretty sure there's at least ten thousand calories in it. It practically melts in your mouth."

I wanted to be strong and say no. I was working at dissolving my baby pooch by sucking it in whenever I remembered and calling it an ab workout. A ten thousand calorie meal wouldn't help with that. Plus, I didn't want Cal and my parents sitting together for a dinner.

But goodness help me, I did want some of Big G's gnocchi and cheese.

I was saved from admitting that I could be bought for gnocchi by my mother saying, "We'd be delighted, Caleb."

"Cal, ma'am."

"Then I'm Judith, Cal."

He chatted for a few minutes with my parents and then promised to come pick us up at six as he left.

"What a nice man," my mother said.

My father nodded.

I glared. "He is not nice."

"Then why are you seeing him?" she asked.

"I'm not." I was going to tell them about Mr. Banning, so I thought fast and said, "We did go out, but I'm just not into him as anything more than a friend."

There that sounded nice, generous even.

"I don't think he sees you as a friend at all," my father said, laughing.

No, he saw me as a suspect. As someone who was obstructing his investigation.

And apparently, he saw me as a dinner date.

Knowing I wasn't going to get anywhere discussing Cal with my parents, I changed the subject. "So what brings you both to town?"

And before they answered, I had my next two questions formulated. *How long are you staying*, and *where are you staying.*

"Don't worry," my mother said. "We're not staying here. Your father's got a conference at The Shelby and we've got a suite."

"I wish you would have let me know you were coming. I'd have taken some time off."

My mother laughed. "No you wouldn't have. You'd have found some excuse not to see us. Over the years, we've learned surprising you is our best bet."

"Mother, I love you both—"

"Oh, sweetie, we know you do. You just don't always enjoy spending time with us. But we're family, so that means you have to." She smiled and then added, "And I should let you know that your brothers and sisters-in-law are attending the same conference. We're all getting together tomorrow night to see your father get his award."

Awards made me think of Mr. Banning and his blood stained Mortie.

My mother gave me her resolute look. I knew I was not only going to dinner tonight with my parents and Cal, I was going to an award banquet tomorrow night.

And somewhere in the midst of all that, I still had to find out, who killed Mr. Banning.

A few hours later, Big G hurried to the door as we arrived. "Cal, Quincy and Mr. and Mrs. Mac. Welcome to my restaurant. I have a table all set up for you."

He sat us in a quiet corner. "And I hope you don't think I'm overstepping, but I decanted the wine for you."

My father tasted the wine with practiced ease and proclaimed it delicious. "We're thinking about heading to Napa after the conference. Judith and I make regular trips to the wineries near our house."

"Where do you live?" Big G asked.

"Erie, Pennsylvania, right on the lake," my father informed him with pride. My father loved my hometown and it showed in his voice.

"There are wineries in Pennsylvania?" Big G asked.

Oh, no, here we go. My father launched into his lecture mode and explained about how the climate at home was comparable to the best wine regions in France, and being on the shores of the Lake Erie helped, too. He talked with passion and he talked with the ease of a teacher. Despite being a medical doctor, my father was a teacher first and foremost. I think it's why his patients loved him. He had a way of explaining a disease or a surgery so that a layperson could understand it and not feel dumb.

After Big G left, the four of us fell into an easy discussion. It went much better than I had thought.

Cal didn't bring up Mr. Banning.

My mother didn't bring up embarrassing stories of my youth.

And the gnocchi and cheese was...

Well, I'd say it was better than sex, but I hadn't had sex in so long, that might be a lie. And given how that kiss with Cal had dazzled me, I suspected sex definitely might be better. But that being said, the gnocchi and cheese was worth some extra work on my baby-pooch.

When we finished the dinner, Big G brought out the tiramisu and I was about to chalk up the dinner as a success, when I became aware of the fact that my father was telling Cal about why he was in town. And the next thing I knew, he was asking Cal to please act as my escort to the award ceremony.

"I don't need an escort, Dad. I'm a mature woman. A business owner. The single mom of three teenaged boys. I'm quite capable of going to a dinner on my own."

"I just thought you'd be more comfortable if you weren't the odd man, or woman as the case may be, out. Your brothers are bringing their wives, I'll be there with your mother. You've come to so many get-togethers on your own. I thought having a date might be a pleasant change of pace."

My father just called me a loser.

I didn't feel like one. I had a good life. I dated on occasion, but hadn't found any man I wanted to keep. Frankly, the three boys were all the Y chromosomes I could take some days.

Most days.

Darn, I missed my boys.

"Whatever," was all I said.

"What she means is she's ecstatic at the prospect of spending a second evening with me," Cal informed my parents.

"Pardon me." I got up from the table and hurried back toward the bathroom. The door was right across from the kitchen door, and I went that way instead and practically walked into Big G, which felt like a fly running into a swatter.

"Problems with my tiramisu?" he asked.

"No. Can I use your office for a few minutes? I need to make a call."

"Sure thing, Quincy." He stopped and stared at me a moment. "So what did Cal do now?"

"Nothing. My parents think he walks on water, to be honest."

"And that's a problem because?"

"He has them believing we're dating. And while I appreciate him not filling them in on my cleaning a crime scene, he's given them false hope. They're eyeing him up as some sort of respectable companion for me. After my ex, they live in fear I'll end up with another Hollywood type."

"Your ex is?" Big G asked.

"A producer. Jerome Smith."

He nodded. "Yeah, I've heard of him."

"Well, they don't approve of him, any more than they approve of me and my career choice."

"Want me to throw the lot of them out? Your parents and Cal? I mean, Cal and I are old friends, but I'm a sucker for a pretty woman."

I stood on tiptoes and kissed his cheek. "You are very gallant, Big G. A true hero. I'll keep the offer in mind."

"Go use my office. If they come looking, I'll tell them you had a business call."

I called the boys.

Hunter picked up. "Hi, honey," I said. "I just called to see how you and your brothers are doing."

He launched into updates on their day's activities, and then passed the phone to Miles, who in turned passed it to Eli.

All in all, not much was said. They were having a great time. They'd been swimming every day. I reminded them to eat some vegetables and use sunscreen.

It wasn't earth shattering, but I felt better and more grounded after connecting with them.

The boys might drive me crazy, but I missed them.

I felt like I was better able to cope with my parents and Cal when I went back to the table. "Sorry. Business call."

"What sort of housekeeping emergency is there at almost eight at night?" my mother asked.

I really don't think she means to sound condescending. I don't believe she thinks she's a snob, but truth is, she does and she is. I glanced at Cal and he looked embarrassed on my behalf.

Most of the time, I let my mother's comments simply zing past me, but having her belittle me in front of Cal made it hard to ignore.

"Mom, I run an important, honest business. It's supported me, the boys, Tiny and all our employees. We do quality work. It might not be brain surgery, but it's honest and what we do is important to the people we work for." I said the words gently, but I saw her register them, then look at Cal, then back at me and finally, at my father.

"I'm sorry," she said. "It's just you could have been anything. You were such a great student, and you could have—"

"Mother, what you mean is, I could have done something else that you could be proud of. Do you remember right after I got that bit part in *Lucky in Love*, you asked me how on earth you could brag to your friends about me being the other-woman in a two bit comedy? Well, here's the thing, Mother, I don't live my life in order for you to have braggable news. You've got the boys for that. Now, if you'll excuse me, I need to get home and get some sleep,

I've got a boring, non-braggable job I need to get to early tomorrow."

"Quincy, I'm sorry."

"I am, too, Mom." I got up and with a great deal of pride, picked up the check. I found Big G. "I know the waitress normally takes this, but could you ring me out?"

He did, and I included a super nice tip, because I knew what it was like to work for tips. Then I waited at the door for my parents and Cal. I wished for my own car to magically appear, but it didn't. I'd ridden with my parents and Cal had driven himself. I could either ride home with my parents like I'd planned, or ask Cal for a lift.

I asked Cal.

My father hugged me goodnight and whispered, "She doesn't mean it."

He'd told me that before, but truth was, she did. She loved me. But she didn't consider me a success by any stretch of the imagination.

"We'll see you tomorrow night," I assured Dad. "Text me the information."

Cal didn't press me for conversation on the ride home. As he pulled into the drive, he turned off the engine and had his hand on the door latch, as if he planned to get out with me.

"Thanks for the ride," I said in such a way I hoped he realized he was not invited inside.

He put his hand back on the steering wheel. "I don't think she meant to be dismissive," he said.

"She did," I assured him. "My uncle went to jail for a crime he didn't commit. He was the lone black sheep of the family until I came along. Uncle Bill and I are the only non-MD's in the family. He went to jail and got a tattoo, and I clean other people's houses. In my mother's eyes, there's not a lot of difference. She loves me, but she can't brag about me to her friends at bridge club, or whatever she does for fun. My doctor brothers and their doctor wives should be enough and they might be, if I had some other job. Being an actress was bad enough, but being a maid is worse."

"Quincy…" Cal didn't say anything else and that was fine because there was really nothing else to say.

"You can always get very busy tomorrow night with some new case if you want to get out of the dinner."

"No. I'm looking forward to it."

"Okay then. Good night." I started to open the door and he reached across the car and caught my arm.

"Really? You're not even going to kiss me goodnight? I mean, it was our second date."

I couldn't help it, I laughed and some of the sadness over my relationship with my mother eased. "It wasn't a date. And we're not going to kiss until after I'm sure you're not going to put me in jail for a murder I didn't commit."

"So, let me be clear, once we find out who really murdered Mr. Banning, we'll be kissing again? We've got a deal?"

I looked at this man and knew what my answer was. "Yes. Deal."

"Well, stop snooping around so I don't have to worry about you, and I'll try and have this case wrapped up in record time." Even in the murky light from the streetlamp, I could see him wiggle his eyebrows in a suggestive way.

I laughed again. "Thanks again, Cal."

"Any time, Quincy. You know, when you're not driving me crazy, I really enjoy being with you."

"Uh, thank you. And ditto."

I got out of the car and hurried inside.

Cal didn't try to follow me.

I wasn't sure if I was happy about that, or disappointed about it.

CHAPTER NINE

LATE THE NEXT AFTERNOON, I stared at my whiteboard. My list of suspects didn't look very, well, suspicious what with the huge X's through them. Not his ex's. Not his daughter. Not his girlfriend.

And today, rather than trying to find some new suspects, I'd done something horrible. Terrible. Frightening beyond belief.

I'd gone shopping with Tiny.

I glanced at the garment bag on the back of the door. I'd survived the shopping trip, but it had been a near thing. I'd barely had time to recover and now, I had another terror to face.

Dinner with my whole family.

A dinner where conversations about medicine were the norm. Where new surgical techniques and diseases were discussed in the same way the boys talked about sports. Since I didn't care much about sports or disease in general, I tended to sit back and let conversation flow around me.

But tonight I'd have a conversation of my own to focus on. A certain murder investigation. Not with my family, but with Cal.

I didn't imagine that he would give me any information freely, but if I could convince him I knew more than I did, maybe something helpful would slip.

First, I need to slip into that dress.

In addition to the dress, Tiny had insisted I buy ... I forget what brand name she used, but I'm going with body-sucker.

Basically, it was a torture device that required me to stuff myself into the spandex horror show in a meat-into-a-sausage-casing sort of way.

I took one last longing look at my whiteboard and unzipped the garment bag.

The color hit me like a glass of cold water after a shock.

Or, given the deep red color of the thing, maybe a glass of wine would be a better analogy.

It was red.

It was slinky in a classy way.

That's how Tiny described it.

I opened the bag on the bed and pulled out the body-sucker and stuffed myself into it. I think my lungs were only capable of filling to half their capacity with it in place. And I was pretty sure that my organs actually shifted their positions because of the pressure. But as I pulled the dress off the hanger and slipped it over my head, it fell light as a feather into place.

I walked over to the mirror.

Tiny was right. The dress was slinky, but in a classy way my mother couldn't object to. And between the body-sucker and dress, my curves seemed sexy, not baby-poochy.

I felt ... pretty.

I put on make-up and flipped my hair into a bun. Tendrils escaped and maybe it was an illusion thanks to the dress, but rather than look messy like it did most days, it looked sexy.

I felt sexy.

I felt more than capable of taking on Detective Caleb Parker.

I paced in the living room, waiting for him.

When the doorbell finally rang, I wanted to sprint to the door, but I didn't want him to think I'd been waiting, so I put on my shoes first, just to complete the look. Then I walked slowly to the door because slowly was the only speed I had when wearing heels and having access to only half-lung breaths.

I opened the door. "Hi, Cal."

He didn't answer.

He didn't move.

He just stared.

He stared in a way that made me forget I was the mother of three teenaged boys. No, his look made feel desirable.

"Cal?" I repeated.

"Uh, Quincy, you're ready."

"Yes, ready on time. I'm punctual." And sexy, I added to myself as a reminder. I was sexy enough to get all kinds of information on the case from Cal.

"Okay, then let's go." He didn't say much as we drove across town, but he kept glancing over at me with a puzzled expression on his face.

When we pulled in at the hotel, he valeted the car. Normally, I just park my car myself and walk, so having it valeted was a treat.

"Come on," he said, giving me another puzzled look.

I stopped. "Is there a problem?"

He gave me an up and down look, the announced, "You look weird."

All my confident, sexy feelings evaporated. "Gee, thanks."

"No, that's not what I meant. You look beautiful but not like you normally do."

"So, normally I don't look beautiful?"

"Normally you look beautiful, but normal. Right now you look..." He must have been thinking about the right phrase because he snapped his fingers and said, "red carpet. You look like some Hollywood actress walking the red carpet."

Now that was actually very nice. Much nicer than *weird.* I felt my confidence return.

"Thanks. You look very nice, too," I assured him. He did. He filled out his suit perfectly.

We headed into the Shelby, which was a beautiful old hotel. Over the years, various owners had added to it, but the newest owner had recently renovated the entryway and reception area back to its original glory.

I suddenly did feel very red-carpety.

Anywhere outside Hollywood might question the word red-carpety as a valid choice, but here, everyone totally understood it.

While Cal checked with one of the desk guys, I stood in the middle of the lobby and simply took in the blue and gold décor.

When I'd moved to LA this is how I pictured my life. Award shows, beautiful old hotels. Red carpet moments.

That's not what I'd gotten, but even though this was beautiful, I was very happy with the life I had.

Well, I would be once I got out of this body-sucker and found Mr. Banning's killer.

Cal interrupted my thoughts. "This way."

"I should probably prepare you. My family is... not normal."

"Whose is?"

"I mean, more than most."

"Your parents seemed nice enough."

"Oh, they are. But... Well, you'll see for yourself. Just remember, there is no escape until after my father wins his award. You're my ride, and I have to stay that long."

STEAMED

"I'm not going anywhere."

We found my parents at one of the head tables. I felt self-conscious as Cal held a chair out to me. My first instinct was to assure him that I was capable of pulling out my own chair, but I looked at my mother and let it slide.

"Cal, you've already met my parents, and this is my brother, Gil and his wife Tanya, and my brother, Art, and his wife, Marie."

Everyone shook and murmured meaningless hellos.

"Dad said you're a cop," Art said, eyeing Cal as if he were a creature in the zoo.

"Yes. A detective, to be precise."

Art nodded, and with that, the conversation moved to some new engineered T cell technology that killed tumors, but not regular cells. Yes, I've hung around with doctor types long enough to have understood that much. But from there the conversation moved into areas that held little interest to me.

No, what did have my interest was Cal's investigation.

So, I turned toward Cal and concentrated on inhaling deeply, which meant my lungs expanded, and since the body-sucker had left so little lung capacity, my breasts expanded, as if to accommodate that extra oxygen. "Can you believe it's only been a week since we've met?"

"It seems like I've known you longer than that," Cal said.

I noticed that his eyes didn't seem to be looking into mine. As a matter of fact, they seemed to be looking a lot lower.

I took another deep breath. "Poor Mr. Banning."

Cal's eyes were definitely looking lower. All this oxygen along with the body-sucker had given me cleavage. "A week and his murder's still unsolved."

"We'll find out who did it," he assured me.

113

I exhaled and inhaled quickly. "It wasn't either of his ex's, his daughter or his girlfriend. That narrows the pool of suspects."

It didn't just narrow my suspects, it eliminated all of them. I wasn't sure where else to look.

"When we find that computer, we'll find the murderer," he said more to himself than me.

I remembered the antiquated computer on the desk by the fireplace. "I saw one on the desk when I was cleaning."

He shook his head. "That was old. According to our techs, he hadn't used it in more than a year. He lived with his laptop. Whatever his new project was, he liked to work on it at the bar on his laptop. You didn't see it at his house, did you?"

He looked at me with a cop-intensity and I had a feeling that no amount of inhaling would phase him.

"No. I didn't see a laptop in the rooms I cleaned. Just some underwear on the ceiling fan and under the sink. I told you that."

"It was his girlfriend's underwear. They'd had a few people over, and afterward..." He smiled suggestively.

I remembered Cassandra's smile as she talked about that last night with Mr. Banning. She'd mentioned his new project and that he liked to work at some bar. That the bartender inspired him.

What if he'd left the laptop at that bar?

Find the computer, find the murderer. And probably find Tiny's pictures.

Find the computer.

In order to do that, I needed to find out where that bar was. There was a chance that's where the computer got left.

That phrase flitted around my head because it was much easier to hold onto than my family's conversation move from T cells to talk of an enzymatic pre-treatment, nanoparticles and biopolymers. It was some new Spanish technique for something medical. Art seemed especially animated about it.

And Art being animated was hard to discern from Art being his normal self-contained self. But as a sister, I could see the difference. I doubted that Cal was going to be able to notice the distinction, especially since his eyes seemed to keep moving in the general direction of my chest.

I breathed in deeply not to gain the upper hand, but to give him a treat. Tomorrow I was back to a sports bra, a Mac'Cleaner's t-shirt and jeans.

"...Dr. Martin Mac," an announcer who I hadn't realized was speaking until that moment said.

My father rose.

He gave a nice speech thanking the organization (I have no idea what medical organization it was) for the recognition and the award. He talked about his new medical procedure, but he might as well have been talking Greek.

He took the trophy and made his way back to the table, and I couldn't help but think of Mr. Banning and his Mortie of death.

I turned to say as much to Cal, when he patted his suit pocket and whispered, "I've got a call. Be right back."

He left me.

With them.

My father's new award was gleaming on the table as people from other tables got up and congratulated him.

My mother was glowing next to him, as if his award cast its luminosity on her.

That left my brothers and their wives.

Rather than basking in my father's medical prowess, they all turned to me in a sort of Stepford Wives synchronicity and Gil said, "So he seems nice. How'd you meet?"

Now, I don't lie. I skirt issues, ignore them or sometimes even blatantly change a subject, but I don't lie.

I tried skirting. "That's some award Dad got, huh?"

"About Cal?"

"Cal and Mal. They rhyme." Okay that was a poor attempt at changing the subject.

"You met him where?"

"After a party." There. That wasn't a lie. Mr. Banning had had some kind of to-do at his house. "He spotted me across the yard and hurried over. He had questions, and I had the answers."

I noticed my sisters-in-laws both smiled at that.

They weren't Macs, so although they were both doctors, they didn't have that same stick-in-the-mud medical myopathy that the Mac DNA seemed to carry. Whenever I visited Erie, they were my respite from Mac-family-overload.

Cal came back to the table, shutting down that particular conversation.

"I've got to go. I've got a new case," he whispered in my ear.

A new case? That meant Mr. Banning's case might fall to the wayside. If it did, Cal might not find the murderer. I didn't want that hanging over my head. And I definitely didn't want the thoughts of the pictures hanging over Tiny's head. I wanted her to enjoy her wedding, every flouncy taffeta minute of it.

"I'll come with you. You can go on your call and I'll catch a cab home."

"I could drop you off."

"Even better."

"Mother. Dad. We have to go. I'm so sorry, but Cal was called out. You all know how it is to have to respond to a call."

They all nodded because they did understand. I don't think I ever had a birthday where at least one of them didn't get called out.

I kissed my father's cheek. "Congratulations, Dad."

"We'll see you in the morning for breakfast," my mother said.

I wondered if I could get called out on a cleaning emergency tomorrow. I waved at the rest of them.

Cal thanked them again for inviting him and we left the ballroom.

The valet brought Cal's car around.

"Sorry to make you leave early."

"Not a problem. Thank you for taking me with you. If you'd left me there, I'd have been surrounded by conversations about T cells and who knows what next. Proctological advances or the like."

He chuckled. "They weren't that bad."

"I know. They're really great and they love me, but the Mac gene doesn't seem to have room for any normal conversations. If I'd asked them what they thought of *The Walking Dead*, I'd have gotten a lecture about how zombies couldn't really exist and even if they did, why would they need to eat human flesh and…"

I laughed, imagining my family discussing the boys' favorite show with all kinds of medical seriousness. "So you saved me from that."

"So, zombies?"

"The boys like the show and I watch it with them. And by watch it, I mean, I follow along and close my eyes for the gory parts. I do like the characters and how they've grown…well, the ones who've survived."

We talked about zombies the rest of the drive. Cal pulled up in front of my house. "I really have to go."

"You're sure it's not something to do with Mr. Banning?"

He shook his head. "No. Like I said, it's a different case. I generally have more than one."

That made sense. On TV, the focus was on one case per episode, but in real life, cops had to multitask because the bad guys didn't take turns with their murders and other crimes.

"Good luck, then," I said. "And thanks for going with me tonight." It had been nice to have a plus-one after years of attending family functions solo, or with just the boys.

"It was my pleasure. And speaking of pleasure, I really wish I wasn't leaving. I'd like to stay."

"But you can't. We can't even repeat that kiss from the other day. Not until after we find the real murderer."

"After that?"

I knew I was smiling like a loon, but I couldn't help it. "After that, we'll see."

"Are there rules about cops kissing suspects goodnight? Just chaste little pecks on the cheek?"

Even the thought of a chaste kiss from Cal sent a shiver up my spine. "Hey, the Europeans do that whole double cheek hello and goodbye kiss all the time, so I guess that's okay."

He leaned forward and I turned my cheek, going for that European sort of goodbye kiss.

Cal bypassed my cheek and went right for my lips.

His lips on my lips.

Uh, I should note that I know chaste kisses and this kiss was not the least bit chaste. It was long. Hard. Intense. And it reminded me I was wearing a slinky red dress and that I was indeed a woman.

And I was very glad I was a woman.

I melted into Cal's embrace, ready to say *yes*. More than that, ready to say *oh-yes*. I was ready to forget he was a cop, and I was a suspect. I was ready to drag him to my bed and have my way with him. And oh, what a *way* it would be.

As I was about to say the words and invite him inside, he pulled back and said, "Well, I'd better go."

For a moment, I wasn't sure my legs would support me. I stumbled a bit. "You're going after that? That wasn't the least bit chaste."

"That little chaste kiss?" There was a twinkle in his eye—it sounded cliché in my head, but that's exactly what it was. The twinkle said he knew without a doubt that the kiss had been anything but chaste. "Sorry, Quincy. I'd love to stay and show you exactly what a real kiss is, but they're waiting for me at a crime scene. I'll talk to you soon."

He turned around and left me without waiting for me to say goodnight. I was left watching him walk back to the car, wishing he were staying to show me the difference between that kiss and his non-chaste one. I wondered if I'd survive a hotter kiss. There was every chance that if it got hotter I might combust.

He waved before he threw his car in reverse and backed out of my driveway.

I let myself in the house, locked the door and then collapsed on the couch.

Finding the computer—more specifically, finding Mr. Banning's laptop.

That was Cal's focus now in Mr. Banning's investigation.

I got off the couch and went to stare at my whiteboard.

I took a sheet of paper and drew a laptop. Okay, so *drew a laptop* was a very generous description. I drew a rectangle. I knew what it was.

I put it in the center of the board.

I took a marker and drew a line to Shaley. She'd mentioned her father calling her *honey*. He'd finished typing, shut his laptop and leaned on it as they talked.

I drew another line to Cassandra. She'd told me that Mr. Banning was working on a new project. He'd take his laptop to some bar with a buffoon bartender and work there.

The laptop wasn't at his house.

He liked to work at the bar.

What if he'd left it there, either by accident or for safekeeping?

I drew a little stick figure. It was Tiny. I didn't want to put her actual picture on the board, because she was not a suspect.

But she was potentially tied to the laptop. I drew a line.

Her pictures could be on it.

So, how to find the laptop? That was my new priority.

Hopefully Cal was going to be distracted for at least a day or two with whatever his new case was.

By the time he was ready to concentrate on Mr. Banning's case again, I'd have the laptop and I'd have erased Tiny's pictures. Afterward, I'd give it to him.

Find the laptop.

Get Tiny's pictures.

Clear my name.

Then find out exactly what one of Cal's non-chaste kisses was like.

CHAPTER TEN

I WOKE UP WITH A START. Someone was knocking on my door.

Everything came back to me in a rush.

My parents.

Dad's award.

Breakfast.

Find the laptop.

Chaste kisses.

It was the kisses part that led to my night of tossing and turning.

I rolled out of bed, tossed on a sweatshirt and wished I hadn't slept in.

I stumbled to the door and greeted my parents with, "Mother. Dad. You're very early."

"It's nearly nine. If we'd come any later, it would have been lunch, not breakfast."

"Maybe we could have tried for brunch?" I muttered.

My father held out a to-go tray. "I brought coffee and donuts."

My mother led the way into the kitchen and was about to take a seat at one of the stools at the counter, when she stopped and brushed off some imaginary crumbs before she sat.

My father simply sat.

I busied myself with getting napkins and plates for the donuts. Finally, there was nothing left to do but sit as well.

"Our flight out is this afternoon," my mother stated. "Your brothers left last night on a red eye."

"Do you need a ride to the airport?" I asked.

"No. I need to know where you and this police officer stand." My mother stared at me in that scientist staring into a microscope sort of way of hers.

I was pretty sure she didn't know that I was a suspect in Cal's case, so I simply said, "He's a detective, and we're friends. We haven't known each other long."

"But you like each other." She nodded, as if she didn't need to wait for me to answer. As if she'd solved some mystery.

I waited for her to tell me he wasn't right for me. That she knew some doctor in Erie who would be perfect for me.

What she said was, "He seems nice, and from the way he was looking at you, the length of time you've known him has very little bearing on his feelings."

"Thank you."

My father quietly munched on his donut and my mother leaned toward me. "I know that sometimes I say things and they come out wrong. I know how to talk to patients. I can deliver bad news and good news with practiced ease. But I've never had any ease when I talk to you."

"Maybe if you'd practice talking and not lecturing on how I'm the family failure."

Dad reached over and took my mother's hand, then shot me a look that said, *Quincy, she's trying.*

I said, "I obviously need some practice, too."

"Then, let's do that. Let's practice. I'll call weekly and we'll talk about my grandkids, about you and Cal, about the family. We'll talk and we'll try."

I took my coffee cup and lifted it toward her.

She smiled, lifted her own cup and toasted mine.

"I'd like that," I said.

"No matter what you think, and no matter what I occasionally say, I'm proud of you, Quincy. You've built a good life for yourself, and you've raised wonderful boys."

"Thank you," I said and I meant it.

My urgent need to find the killer—or at the very least Mr. Banning's computer—grew. I didn't want to lose whatever ground I'd just gained with my mother.

More than anything, I wanted her to find someway to be proud of me. And going to jail for murder wasn't the way to make that happen.

Sunday was quiet. I spent an hour and a half talking to the boys ... and Peri. She always liked to say hi.

I read the paper in bed.

I drank an entire carafe of coffee.

I finished cleaning the house. That way if the cops did show up to arrest me and had a search warrant, I wouldn't die of maidly embarrassment.

But mainly, I pondered.

I tried to decide how to find out what bar was Mr. Banning's inspiration and workplace.

Cassandra Yu was my link.

I just had to decide how to get to her without seeming creepy.

I baked some cookies.

I don't want to brag, but my oatmeal cookies are so good that people who don't even like oatmeal like them.

That's why Monday morning before I even went to the office, I pulled into Cassandra's driveway.

I figured it was early enough that I'd catch her before work. Her car was in the drive.

I 'accidentally' hit the horn as I got out of the car with my giant plate of cookies.

Cassandra opened her front door.

"Oh, I'm so sorry, Ms. Yu. I was just going to leave these on your porch."

"What is it?" she asked. She looked a little better than last week. As if she'd managed to get some sleep.

"Cookies. I felt so bad about your loss that I thought I'd leave some comfort food."

"Really, you didn't have to—"

"There's a saying—*I don't have to do anything but die and pay taxes.* I try to live by that. So rest assured, I wanted to." And really, despite the fact I was using her for information, I did want to do something to ease her pain. "Losing someone is hard. Cookies don't really help but they'll remind you that someone cares."

"Why don't you come in and have a cup of coffee and a cookie with me. I mean, never mind. You're probably on your way to work."

"I've got time. Just let me lock my car." Now, that was a brilliant touch. Leave my purse in the unlocked car, as if I was planning to get back in right away.

I handed Cassandra the plate, dug for my keys, which as always had disappeared to the bottom of my mom-purse and hit the lock button on the fob.

We went into the kitchen and Cassandra poured me a cup of coffee. I occasionally thought about cutting back on my coffee intake. I mean, there was a chance I had a slight addiction going.

But really, I kept it under four cups a day. Okay, sometimes a few more.

Okay, sometimes a lot more.

But if you're going to be addicted to something, I figured coffee wasn't a bad option.

Of course, there was a chance I could become addicted to Cal's chaste-kisses and really would like a chance to experience, and possibly become addicted to his non-chaste ones, too.

"So, how are you?" I asked Cassandra.

"Better," she said weakly. "The funeral was hard. His ex's were both there, and his daughter. Shaley came over to me and hugged me. She said I'd made her father happy. I didn't expect that. She's been cold to me in the past. She seemed ... different somehow."

"Different good?" I asked with no private investigator interest. I genuinely liked the girl.

"Yes. I mean she was telling me she's got a job as a cater-waiter to help pay her tuition. She's Steve's sole heir, but it's going to take a long time to sort that out, so in the meantime, she's working."

"It's nice to see kids grow up and become responsible."

"It is." She lowered her voice as if someone could hear. "We're going out next week. I have a friend who's a genius with hair, and Shaley could use the help."

"That's nice. It's nice you both had each other to lean on at the funeral. I hope a lot of his friends showed up."

"Oh, they did. It was like a Hollywood A-List gathering. Even his ex-writing partner, Louis Michaels was there."

"He didn't see his partner often?" I asked.

Cassandra shook her head. "No, Lou and Steve had a falling out over a project and broke up about the same time Steve divorced Tessa."

The ex-writing partner? Could he be a suspect? Mr. Banning obviously knew him. Knew him well enough to let him into the house.

"And I finally met his bartender friend."

"What bartender friend?" I asked absently, my mind was still focused on Louis Michaels. He could be the killer. A man would be strong enough to hit Mr. Banning with his Mortie... strong enough to bludgeon him to death.

"The bartender friend Steve based his new show's main character after. *Hanky Panky*, he named it. Steve pitched it as *Cheers* meets *Arsenic and Old Lace*. The bartender was a slime-ball all right. Steve didn't make that up."

"What did he do?"

"He hit on me at my boyfriend's funeral." She lowered her voice. "*Stop in at the bar, sweetheart. We don't get many lookers and you'd class up the joint.*"

Don't get many lookers.

That struck a chord.

It took me a minute, but then I said, "This wouldn't be Willy from The Bit Part Bar, would it?"

She nodded. "Yes. How did you know?"

"I stopped there one day to get a Guinness. It had a lot of... character."

Cassandra laughed at that. "That's what Steve used to say. He'd stopped in there for years. His ex-wife lives in the neighborhood, and it was convenient. He liked the shabby atmosphere, but it was the bartender who really inspired him with this new series."

"How did his ex-writing partner feel about his success?" I asked.

"Louis works for the studio these days. I think he was genuinely happy for Steve. They had lunch a few months back and cleared up whatever their past issues were."

She didn't know what they were? "So they were friends again?"

She shook her head. "I think they were friendly. They were both in very different places, but Louis was truly broken up about Steve's murder."

Was he really broken up about Mr. Banning's murder, or could he feel guilty about murdering him?

Mr. Banning was killed with his Mortie. A Mortie he won for writing. Writing he used to do with Louis Michaels.

Could it be jealousy? Or some remnants of their falling out?

Was it coincidence that after years of estrangement, they'd finally gotten back together and right after that, Mr. Banning was killed?

Questions and theories flitted through my mind as Cassandra and I talked. We made arrangements to get together in a week for dinner.

I hugged her as I left. I might not have found Mr. Banning's murderer yet, but I was pretty sure I'd found a new friend.

And that thought made me feel guilty. I should have told Cassandra what I was up to.

I immediately decided that no, I shouldn't have. If Cal questioned her he might find out.

Thoughts of prisons and wrinkled unicorns confirmed I did the right thing not mentioning it. But after I'd found Mr. Banning's killer, I'd tell Cassandra the whole story.

I thought about stopping at the bar, but my cellphone rang and I pushed the button on the steering so I could answer hands free.

"Quincy, Theresa called in again. I need you at the office while I take over her route."

"We're going to have to fire Theresa," I said as I whizzed by The Bit Part Bar. I'd go back there tonight.

❧ ❧ ❧

Office duty was no picnic. I took calls, dealt with employees, and fielded a bunch of Tiny's wedding calls.

There was enough work that I was busy, but not so much that I couldn't think about the computer and *Hanky Panky's* inspiration The Bit Part Bar.

Maybe Mr. Banning's laptop was there and if it was there, maybe I could get my hands on it. I could tell Cal and trust that he could get it, but I didn't want him to get it while there was a good chance that's where Tiny's pictures were.

I doubted very much that the slimy bartender would give it to me just because I asked, but I could offer to buy it.

I thought about grabbing a checkbook, but in the end, went out and got a thousand dollars cash from the bank next door.

If Mr. Banning had left his laptop at the bar, odds are the slimy bartender planned on keeping it since Mr. Banning was dead.

I'd offer to pay him cash.

There was a very good chance that the laptop wasn't at the bar. And that led me back to my brick wall.

But I had a new lead. Louis Michaels.

The cops always looked at family members and lovers first as suspects in a murder.

I would think that a writing partner was as close as a relative.

What would *The Closer* do?

She'd ask one of her men to do some kind of background search on Louis Michaels in her very polite Southern way and they'd find some tiny, almost random sounding fact that would break the whole case open. Then they'd arrest

STEAMED

him and Brenda would do her *Closer* kind of stuff and get him to confess and win the day.

Maybe there was something on the computer that could prove that Louis was the murderer and if not him, maybe it would point to who was.

Once I had the computer, I could delete Tiny's pictures, look for more clues, and after that, I'd turn it over to Cal.

Yeah, that's right. I'd turn it over. I want to find out who murdered Mr. Banning so I didn't end up on death row—if California had one. And while I felt I was pretty good at this whole investigating thing, Cal was probably better at it than I was. He did it professionally.

I cleaned houses professionally.

Yeah, I'd put my money on Cal having a better chance at figuring it out than me.

But that being said, I wasn't willing to trust him so much that I would stay out of things.

Uncle Bill had believed that because he was innocent things would work out.

And I guess they did... eventually.

I didn't want to hang out in prison waiting for that eventuality.

I did a websearch on Louis Michaels.

Hollywood Action gave me a start and a few phone calls to friends in the business, gave me the rest of the information I needed. I'd been so close to him and I hadn't even known it.

I called Honey Martin at Le Celebre.

I had an idea.

I'd just hung up from talking to Honey when the phone rang and I picked it up. "Mac'Cleaners. We do it all and we're glad you made the call. This is Quincy. How may I help you?"

129

"Quincy, it's Cal."

"Why are you calling me at work?"

"I thought I could see you tonight."

"I don't think that would be wise, especially after that uh, chaste kiss. I'm a suspect, remember?"

"You're not a suspect, you're a witness. But yeah, we can't be kissing again, until after I close this case. But there's nothing wrong with my quizzing you again about the murder scene … over dinner."

"No. And even if I wanted to, I can't. I have plans."

"What plans?" He sounded suspicious.

"Is that Cal the cop asking, or Cal the man who kissed my socks off?"

"First, that kiss was chaste. As soon as I've solved this case, I'll show you a real kiss. Secondly, Cal the cop and Cal the kisser are the same man. I'm asking."

"Well, I find both Cal's intrusive. I don't owe you an explanation. It's Monday, and you're killing my Monday glee."

"Monday glee?"

"I like Mondays."

He snorted.

"I do. They're an underappreciated day. I have a writer friend who's convinced me that Mondays should get some love. So, I try to. But you're making it tough. I've got to go."

I hung up.

I had a plan, I had a suspect in my sites, and I had at least a potential place Mr. Banning might have left his computer.

Not a bad day in the amateur detective world.

Tiny called in when she'd finished the last house. I did some more online surfing and then headed over to Le Celebre.

Honey left a supply closet on the fourteenth floor open and in it was a smock that the hotel cleaning service people wore.

I put on the smock, took a cart and went to room 1488. Now, here's the thing, despite what the room numbers said, this wasn't really the fourteenth floor. It was the thirteenth. A lot of hotels eliminated a thirteenth floor because so many guests balked at staying on them. I've always felt a fake fourteen was even more suspect than a thirteenth one that owned its thirteenth, at least luck-wise. I was hoping that it wouldn't be my luck that was comprised.

I hoped that any unluckiness was for Louis Michaels.

I tried to channel everything Mr. Magee had taught me in acting school. Then I gave myself a little mental pep talk. How hard could acting like a hotel maid be? I was a maid by trade.

Still going into a strange man's room, a man I thought had some motive for murder, was a bit more daunting than I'd thought.

I thought of Uncle Bill, of my boys and of wrinkled unicorns. I knocked on the door. "Maid service," I announced.

"Come in."

Shoot.

I was hoping against hope that he wasn't in. I wanted a chance to ransack the room in peace.

Still, in for a penny, in for a pound.

I opened the door and propped my cart against it, holding it open.

I didn't see Louis Michaels in the murky room. The curtains were drawn.

"Hi," I said to the room in general. "Just came in to change your towels and see if you needed anything."

A bedside lamp turned on.

Propped against a pile of pillows on the bed was a small man.

I wasn't sure about his height. Wasn't there a saying that all men are the same height when they're lying down?

Or is it laying down?

I can never keep that lay/lie thing straight.

Thinking about grammar was easier than thinking about the fact I was in a room with a potential killer.

"You're new," he said, his words slurred.

"I'm just a temp."

I got a stack of towels from the cart and went into his bathroom. The towels there were clean, but I replaced them anyway.

"Is there anything else you need, sir?" I asked.

"I need some more whiskey. Any chance you'd get me some? Room service will bring me a glass, but I want a bottle. A bottle of the good stuff."

"That would be against the hotel's policy, sir." That was a guess, but I'm pretty sure if not breaking the hotel's monopoly on room service wasn't a policy, it should be. "But I'm off work in a few minutes, sir. If I were to go out and buy a bottle, then bring it up to a friend's room, well, that's just one friend hanging out with another."

"Would you do that?" he asked with a drunken hitch in his voice.

"Sure. I'll be back in less than half an hour."

I hurried out of the room, returned the cart and uniform to the closet, went down the street and picked up a bottle, and was back at Mr. Michael's door in twenty minutes.

I knocked. He hollered to come in. "I don't have a key anymore, sir. I'm just a friend visiting a friend."

I heard a lot of stumbling, and then he opened the door. "You came back."

"I did. And I brought—" I held the bag aloft.

"Come in and have a drink with me."

That same trepidation was there. I was going, willingly, into the room of someone I thought could have committed murder.

I went anyway.

A mother can find all kinds of bravery when it comes to her kids, and my kids needed me free, not in jail.

A friend could find all kinds of bravery when it came to her friends. Tiny deserved to be happy and that meant finding those pictures.

I went in.

Mr. Michaels shut the door.

"I'll get the glasses."

He pulled two plastic wrapped glasses from the hotel tray on the desk.

While he unwrapped them and set them up, I got out the bottle of Jameson.

"An Irish girl?" he asked.

I handed him a glass. "Yes."

"My friend who died, he was Irish. To Steve."

I raised my glass. "To Steve," I echoed. I sipped my whiskey. "What happened, if you don't mind my asking?"

"Someone murdered him. He was a bastard sometimes, but we came up through the ranks together. We were partners for years. And now he's gone. It just goes to show how precarious life is. One minute you're here, working, loving, just living life, and the next…whack. Someone bludgeons you to death."

"They bludgeoned him?" I didn't have to pretend to be horrified at the thought—the image of him was burned in my brain and every time I thought of it, there was plenty of real horror on my part.

"With his own Mortie. He was so damned proud of that award. He said this new project he was working on was going to get him another." He laughed bitterly, raised his glass, then downed the rest of the contents without saying a word.

He extended the glass to me. "Sir, I think you've had enough," I said.

"Call me Louis. Or Lou. You should know the name of the man you're drinking with. And you are?"

I thought about lying, but I was pretty sure this man wasn't my murderer, so I said, Quincy."

"Quincy, nice to meet you. Now, pour me another glass. And if you go into the desk drawer, there's a stack of money. Take enough to pay for the bottle."

"That's fine, sir. I'm sure Mr. Banning would like that we were drinking to him."

He set the glass down. "How did you know his last name was Banning? I'm pretty sure I just called him Steve."

I am not the most brilliant member of the Mac family, but I've always been a bit of a black sheep, which means that on more than one occasion in my misbegotten youth, I had to think fast in order to stay out of trouble.

"You said your friend was Steve and he was bludgeoned with a Mortie. I read about Mr. Banning in the paper. And frankly, I've seen coverage on the news. It's a big story." There. That was the truth, but of course, not all of it.

"Oh. Yes. Of course." He took the bottle and poured his own glass. "To Steve."

I raised my glass and toasted.

It was after nine when I left the rather inebriated Mr. Michaels in bed. I'd hidden the bottle in his desk drawer, next to his pile of untouched money. The alcohol was my treat.

I went back to the kitchen and found Honey. "Just wanted to say thanks for the help."

She gave me a accessing look. "How much did you drink?"

"Just a few glasses of whiskey."

"Did you find out what you needed to find out?"

I nodded, which made the room shift slightly on its axis. I grabbed the counter to steady myself.

"When's the last time you ate?"

"I had some yogurt at lunch."

She tsked. "Really, sometimes friends are more trouble than kids. Sit down and I'll get you dinner."

"I really have to go. I have another appointment."

"Quincy, we're friends. You and Tiny gave me a job when I was in school and were so great about working around my schedule. I'm enough of a friend to tell you that if you try to get behind the wheel right now, I'm calling the cops. But after they hauled you away, I promise, I'd come bail you out."

Honey might be younger than me. I might have helped her out back when she was in school. But she was a mom now. And it showed.

I sat.

She fed me this awesome chicken dish and made me drink two glasses of water and then coffee.

An hour and a half later, the room no longer tilted on its axis, my baby pooch was overflowing my waistband and I had to pee.

I was definitely sober as I left the kitchen and headed across town to The Bit Part Bar.

I left the kitchen knowing that Mr. Michaels hadn't killed Mr. Banning. He was too genuinely torn up. And frankly, I wasn't sure his tiny frame had enough umph to swat a fly, much less bludgeon a man of Mr. Banning's adequate size.

I'd have to go home, print out a picture of Lou then put an X through it. Yet another suspect unsuspected.

Maybe one of my now unsuspected suspects had really done it and my mom-senses were off. But if I was right, I'd need to find someone else to look at.

I thought of all my cop show favorites. I hit a bit of a speed bump as I thought about *Castle* and Nathan Fillion. If I didn't have Cal in my life, I might have lingered on thoughts of Nathan Fillion a bit longer, but thinking of finding Mr. Banning's murderer and getting back to kissing Cal made me push past my girl-crush on Castle.

Who else would want to kill poor Mr. Banning?

What did I know?

It was someone he knew well enough to let in his house.

It was someone big enough to actually bludgeon him.

That was it.

I'd have to go back online and do more research.

But first, I needed to see if the computer was at the bar.

CHAPTER ELEVEN

I HEADED TO THE BIT PART BAR.

It didn't look merely shabby in the dark, it looked seedy.

For a moment, I worried about finding a parking space at eleven at night, but it turned out the parking lot was almost empty.

I was pretty sure that state law required bars close by two. Last call was one thirty.

I'd have a couple hours to try and see if Mr. Banning's computer was somewhere. I remembered seeing the bartender on a laptop when I'd stopped in and had my Guinness.

Though the bar was almost empty, I sat down at the far end of the bar. The seat gave me a good vantage point to watch the three other drinkers in the bar.

The bartender came over.

"Guinness, wasn't it?" he asked when he saw me.

"You remember me?" I was surprised.

"I never forget a pretty face," he said with a slimy leer. "You brighten up the place."

I didn't know what to say to that, so I simply said, "Thank you." My mother always said, when in doubt be polite. "And yes, a Guinness."

He ambled to the other end of the bar and took his time pouring my Guinness right. We Macs appreciate someone who can pour a Guinness well.

He came back and gave me what I think was supposed to be a suggestive look. "So, you enjoyed the atmosphere of the bar, or me?"

"It's convenient. I have friends who live in the area. Cassandra Yu? She said her boyfriend used to come work here."

That stopped him. He studied me. His eyes narrowed. He leaned on the bar and bent closer. "You know Cassandra's boyfriend?"

"No. I just know she's been broken up because she lost him. And she mentioned he liked to come work here."

"Oh, he did."

"He said the bar was an inspiration. He was working on a project, but Cassandra said she can't find his computer. It's not at her place, and it wasn't as his." I called on all my Mr. Magee inspired acting skills and brightened my expression. "By any chance did he leave it here?"

Willy leaned a bit further, encroaching on my personal space in a very uncomfortable way. His expression was bordering on scary. Suddenly he smiled. "Why are we talking about Steve? Let's talk about you and me."

I laughed as if he were telling me a joke. "Thanks for the beer. You do pour a great Guinness."

"Tell you what, if you wait around a bit and when the bar clears out, I'll see if I can find the computer in the lost and found. You'd never believe all the things people leave behind in a bar."

"Thank you. I know Cassandra would love to have it. There were pictures of the two of them on it that she'll have lost forever if she doesn't find it." And hoping to convince him the thought was spontaneous, I added, "I'm so glad I thought to mention it. He always had so many nice things to say about the bar and everyone in it."

Willy drew back and I felt overwhelmingly relieved that there was the barrier of distance between us. He smiled and said, "I'll definitely check. You never know what someone's put in the lost and found box. And I have a few stories I could tell you about good old Steve. Stories his girlfriend might want to hear."

"That would be lovely."

What would be really lovely was finding the laptop and getting out of here. Willy was an odd duck.

My phone buzzed in my purse. I went fishing and found it…at the bottom. Everything I wanted was always at the bottom of my purse.

It was a text from Cal. *Where are you?*

Why? I replied.

I'm on your porch.

I'm not at home.

I know that now. Where are you? Are you investigating?

I'm doing something for a friend. I won't be home until late.

My phone rang, and it was Cal.

I pressed the button on the top and sent the call to voicemail.

When the phone buzzed to tell me there was a message I picked it up. "*Quincy, I know you're investigating. Don't. It's dangerous. I don't want to see you get hurt.*"

I hung up the phone and within seconds it buzzed again, telling me I had another voice message. "*And if you're not back home in the next half hour, I'm putting out an APB and bringing you down to the station for questioning. That's right, Quince. I'll have the police haul you into the station, and I'll hold you as a material witness.*"

I texted him. *Bite me.*

It definitely wasn't the mature response. It wasn't the response I'd encourage my boys to use, but it felt good.

Thinking of Cal biting me…tiny little love nips as we finally got together for real and I got to discover just what one of his non-chaste kisses was like kept my mind fully occupied for the next hour as I nursed my Guinness and wait for the bar to clear out.

Maybe Willy would have the computer, and then I'd call Cal when I got home. Well, I'd call him after I removed Tiny's pictures. It would be just what he needed to figure out who killed Mr. Banning. And after he found the murderer, we'd…

"That's it. They're all gone."

I glanced at the clock. "I figured they'd all be here until last call."

"I kicked them out."

"You checked the lost and found for the laptop?" I asked hopefully.

He held up an orange colored laptop case. "It was here. Someone put it in a desk drawer, probably because they knew it was Steve's. I didn't know it was here."

That was a lie. It was the same laptop I'd seen Willy working on the first time I visited the bar.

He stared at me with an off-putting intensity.

"Well, I'm relieved for Cassandra's sake. I'll see to it she gets it tomorrow."

I held out my hands, expecting him to hand it to me.

Instead, he walked around the bar and came down to my end and sat on the barstool next to me. "Did you know anything about what he was working on?" he asked.

I shook my head. "I just know Cassandra said The Bit Part Bar was the inspiration."

He set the laptop on the bar and leaned towards me again. "He told me the same thing. He came in here day after day and worked at that booth." He pointed to the last booth against the front wall. "He'd watch me work, watch the people come in throughout the day and he'd type away. His hands flew on the keyboard. *Willy, I'll be sure to mention the bar when I win my next Mortie for this,* he'd say."

"That was nice," I offered, eyeing the laptop. I wanted nothing more than to grab it and leave.

"That's what I thought. Then one day, his ex-wife called about his daughter and her school. Some problem with the kid's tuition. He went on and on, saying how much he loved her and how he hated letting her down again. He ran out and forgot the laptop. I was curious. So, after he left, I started to read what he wrote."

Willy's face was red, his eyes were bugging out. He looked furious and for the first time I wasn't just a bit uncomfortable around the slimy bartender, I was scared. I reached in my pocket and pushed the button that turned the volume all the way down, then turned the phone on. I knew that the last person who'd called was Cal. He'd left a message I'd listened to. I tried to remember what to push in order to redial. I prayed I did it right. I tried to picture my voicemail screen. The call back button was on the bottom left…I thought.

I pushed that area and hoped I was right.

Willy's eyes were glazed as if he was back at that moment, reading Mr. Banning's script. They focused again, but were wild as they looked at me. "He'd written a script about a bar. And a bartender."

"I guess you were the inspiration, Willy. You and The Bit Part Bar." I was impressed I'd worked that into the conversation. If I'd manage the redial correctly, Cal was listening.

He'd know where I was. "It must have made you happy that you and The Bit Part Bar here would be known as his inspiration," I added loudly just in case Cal didn't hear me the first time.

"The bartender in the script was a moron. A slimy, womanizing jerk. He was a buffoon. And as I read it, I realized that's how he saw me. Steve saw me as a creepy man who spent his days trying to pick up women and never succeeding."

I thought it wise not to comment that Mr. Banning's assessment was right on the money. "I'm sorry."

"So was he," Willy said ominously. "I called Sherm to cover the bar and I took the laptop to good old Steve's house that night. I was going to tell him that he couldn't sell that script. I got there and parked in front of his house. I saw his girlfriend leave. I waited until she was out of sight, then I walked across the grass and went to the door.

"Steve opened it and smiled. He invited me and thanked me for bringing his laptop. I realized I'd tracked in mud from the grass and took off my boots. Steve laughed and said it was all right. Everything was going to be all right."

"But it wasn't," I whispered. The footprints I'd steamed. They were Willy's.

"No, it wasn't all right. Steve told me he'd had a huge fight with his ex about his daughter's tuition and that his girlfriend had made him feel so much better. He said this new girlfriend was the one. He said he'd been married twice, and thought he'd loved another woman once. The wives divorced him and the other woman was getting married to someone else. Personally, I think good old Steve had too many women in his life. But he kept telling me this new one was special. She was different. They'd had a couple friends over, and when the friends left, she'd made him feel better." Willy snorted. "Yeah, I know what that means. That's why the other women who betrayed him, his wives, his daughter and the lady he'd loved who was marrying someone else didn't bother him. He had a new woman in his bed."

Willy shook his head in disgust. "If you ask me, all women are the same." I wanted to assure him I wasn't asking. I realized the woman-getting-married that Mr. Banning had talked about had to be Tiny. I doubted Mr. Banning had destroyed her pictures, but odds are he was that head-over-heels for Cassandra he hadn't done anything with them. That was good news.

I looked at Willy's crazed face … it was not good news. I hoped Cal was listening to this. I knew I needed to get Willy to say what he'd done. So, I asked, "What else did Steve say?"

"He said the script was about ready to go and he was sure it was going to be a hit."

Willy zoned out, but his expression was even scarier. Suddenly I didn't want to get him to confess to anything. I just wanted to go home.

"I should be going, Willy," I said.

I'd explain about the pictures to Cal. He'd understand and make sure they didn't leak. There's no way he'd think Tiny did it, not when whacko Willy was saying he'd gone there that night after Cassandra left.

I started to stand, but Willy reached across the bar and grabbed my wrist. "No, you should hear the rest of this. I told Steve that I'd read the script and that he had to change it. The bartender was nothing like me. He laughed at me. Laughed. At. Me. And then he said that it was too late. He'd talked to some friends about *Hanky Panky* and there was interest. He was sure the show would put The Bit Part Bar on the map. I screamed at him. I told him to keep the bar, but he had to change the bartender. I'd be a laughing stock.

"He laughed and said, *Calm down, Willy. Let me get you a drink.* And when he turned his back on me to get the drink, I took his Mortie—his precious Mortie—and I hit him. He ran toward his bedroom then, shouting at me to cut it out. *Change it*, I screamed. *Change the script.* He grabbed his cell-phone off his bed and dialed. I cornered him and hit the phone out of his hand. Then I hit him again. And again. And…Next thing I knew, he was sprawled on the bed and it was obvious he was dead. I don't remember doing it. I didn't want him dead, I just wanted him to fix the script." He sounded positively perplexed. He'd just wanted a script changed, so why was Mr. Banning dead?

Then a realization hit me. Whacko Willy had just confessed to the murder in a television interrogation worthy moment.

Only problem was, this wasn't TV. And I wasn't a detective. I was a mom. I was a maid. And I was alone in a bar with a crazy man who'd just confessed he'd murdered someone.

"Willy, it was an accident," I tried. I just wanted to get out and get away from this crazy man. "Mr. Banning shouldn't have written that. You're not like that."

He was shaking his head and looking muttering, "Hit him. Hit him. I hit him."

"It'll all be fine, Willy. I won't say anything to anyone." I reached in my pocket and touched my phone, praying that Cal got my message and was on his way. "No one will ever know."

"No. No one can ever know. They'd lock me up and I'd get the needle."

"Does California have a death penalty? I've been wondering that lately and haven't found time to look it up."

He ignored my question. "No, I don't want to get locked up so no one else can know."

"And I won't tell," I promised.

"You might, so I'm sorry, but you can't leave."

I bolted from my stool and headed for the door. Willy leaped over the bar and was on my heels and grabbed my arm. "You can't leave."

"Let me go," I screamed and hit him in the face with a fist. And because I had boys, I remembered to keep my thumb on the outside so I didn't break it. But the rest of my fingers felt like they might be broken.

"I can't let you go," he said.

I'd read an article once that said make yourself a person to an abductor. Help them identify with you. "I'm a mom. A single mom. I've got three boys. And I wouldn't want anyone to make fun of them in a TV show. I'm on your side, Willy. Bullying is wrong."

"Oh, it was wrong, but now no one will ever know. You're not leaving."

There was a sound outside and Willy turned toward it, and at that moment, I kicked him in the crotch with all my might. He dropped my arm and fell to the floor, cradling himself.

The door to the bar opened and Cal came in.

"You got my message?" I asked.

He nodded, without taking his eyes off Willy. "Police ..."

"Owwwwww," Willy moaned.

Cal walked over, grabbed Willy's hand and flipped him onto his stomach, grabbed the other and cuffed him.

Once he was handcuffed, he said, "Backup should be here any moment."

He pulled Willy to his feet and dragged the still moaning man toward the door.

I saw the laptop, still sitting on the bar next to my purse. My giant, oversized mom-purse.

While Cal and Willy were at the door watching for the backup, I ran over, grabbed the computer, stuffed it in my purse and walked back to the door with Cal and Willy.

"I just wanted him to rewrite the character," Willy whined.

"You just wanted to kill me to keep me quiet," I said, winding up my foot for another kick.

"Down, Tiger. We've got him. He confessed to you, so we've got a witness. Willy, if you're smart, you'll make a deal with the DA and not take this to trial because we've got your dead to rights."

Suddenly Cal looked at me, "And you. You and I are going to talk about this as soon as we get your statement."

"Fine. I'd like to … talk."

"I told you I'd find out who did it," Cal said.

"I didn't need you to find out. I did it myself."

Suddenly the realization sank in. I wasn't going to prison. I wasn't getting a unicorn tattoo that was sure to wrinkle in a few years. My boys wouldn't have to go live with their father and Peri.

I patted my purse and felt the outline of the laptop. And I had the computer, which meant, I had Tiny's pictures, I hoped.

Cal insisted I ride with him to the station.

That was fine with me. I'd had a third drink of the evening, and I'd almost been killed. I shouldn't be behind a wheel.

"Cal, I—"

"Be quiet, Quincy. We're going to book Willy on murder, then we're going to take your statement. After that, I'm taking you home."

"And then?" I asked, because I wanted more than Cal taking me home and then leaving.

"And then we're going to have a serious discussion about amateur sleuths and what obstruction of justice means."

I sighed. I figured as much.

"And then?" I asked hopefully.

Cal growled.

I didn't see much chance for more kissing—chaste or non-chaste—in my immediate future.

Darn it all.

Chapter Twelve

THE NEXT DAY, I went into the office and gave Tiny the thumb-drive with her pictures on it. "I looked, just to make sure it was the right file, but I kept my eyes closed after that and just cut and pasted. I called Hunter and he told me how to scrub the hard-drive so there's no versions of the pictures left. If someone really went looking, they might find it, but I don't think that's going to happen. I didn't want to totally wipe the drive, because I wanted Cassandra to have the laptop. I don't think anyone will be looking for these."

Tiny hugged me. "Thank you, Quincy. I took your advice and told Sal. He laughed and said he'd seen my body, so if the pictures did show up, there'd be nothing he hadn't seen before. He loves me. He's..."

"Perfect," we said in unison.

Tiny said not to worry about work the rest of the day, so I went to see Shaley at Honey's. I told Shaley what Willy had said about her dad. He loved her, and he felt horrible about her tuition.

She told me that she'd seen the lawyer and could go back to school in the fall, but she was going to work the rest of the last few weeks of summer anyway.

Finally, I went to Cassandra's. I confessed everything to her and pulled the computer out of my bag. "I probably should have given this to the cops, but they had Willy's confession so they don't need it. I thought you might want the pictures."

"A producer friend of Steve's called to ask about the script he'd been working on. I didn't know where it was. But with this…Well, if it sells, Shaley will have the money toward school."

She took the laptop and hugged it to her chest as she broke into tears. "Thank you, Quincy."

"I'm sorry I lied to you, but I needed to be sure you didn't do it."

She smiled. "I loved him."

"I know. That's why there's a giant X through your picture on my whiteboard.

"Tell me everything from the beginning," she instructed.

I did. The only thing I glossed over was finding Mr. Banning in the bedroom and Tiny's pictures.

"And Willy confessed. The district attorney worked out a deal. He's going to be in jail for the rest of his life, but she took the death penalty off the table."

California did have one.

Darn, that was a close call. If I hadn't found the real murderer, I could have ended up on death row.

But I knew that wouldn't have happened. Cal wouldn't have let it. He was mad at me—that much was clear last night as he read me the riot act. But I didn't think he'd have been that mad if he didn't care. And I knew that he'd have found Willy without my help.

I was glad he didn't have to. I felt empowered having found the killer on my own. Oh, maybe it was dumb luck, or beginner's luck. It doesn't matter what you called it, I'd found the murderer. I didn't even need Cal to save me from Willy's attack. I'd flattened the crazy bartender with one good kick.

HOLLY JACOBS

I left Cassandra's with a date for coffee next week and a new client for Mac'Cleaners. But most importantly I'd found a new friend.

I drove to Big G's.

"Hi, beautiful," Big G said when I walked in.

"Is he here?" I asked.

"In the back."

"What's his mood like?"

"Well, let's just say he's a little less than his normal sweetness and light self."

"Oh," That didn't sound good. Not good at all.

Big G hugged me. "It will be okay. I heard what happened. He's just worried. He keeps thinking about what could have happened. I'll confess, I've thought of that, too."

He pulled back from the hug and said, "Don't ever do something like that again. But I'm glad you could handle yourself."

"It might have been better if I hadn't taken the suspect down on my own. If Cal had rescued me, he might not be so mad."

"Quincy, I know we've only just met, but I suspect we're going to be good friends, and I'm going to trade in against that future friendship and say, never be less than who you are for a man. Not any man. If they can't accept you're a competent woman who's capable of saving yourself, then $#%$ them." Yes, he said that word I won't let me boys say. "That being said, don't put yourself in harms way again."

I bleeped his F-bomb out in my own head. I kissed the big man's cheek. "Thanks, Big G. I'll try not to."

"Good. Because if you ever pull a stunt like that again, I'll hold you down while Cal wallops you like you'd wallop one of your kids."

"I never hit my kids, and you and what army," I said as a retort. He laughed and took me to a back table where Cal sat glowering at me.

Big G beat a quick retreat without so much as a here's-today's-specials.

"Cal, I—" I was going to say that while I wouldn't apologize for solving the case, I was sorry I made him worry and I was really sorry if he looked bad at work because I'd caught Willy.

I didn't get to say anything. "Don't talk about it," he snapped.

"But I—"

"Really, Quince. This is our first official date. You're not a suspect, I'm not investigating a murder. A murder that's been solved. The killer's going to jail. The DA thinks he'll plead guilty at the preliminary hearing. They're working on that deal. So, I'm going to concentrate on that, not on the fact that you did all that amateur sleuthing and almost got yourself killed by a whack job. I'm going to drink some wine. Eat pasta and afterward, I'm going to take you home and show you what a non-chaste kiss is like."

Suddenly, I wanted to eat the quickest meal ever and get to the home and kissing part. I took a long drink of wine.

And then ate the fastest meal ever.

We went home and I discovered Cal was right when he'd said that other kiss was practically chaste. His non-chaste kiss nearly caused me to self-combust.

I was glad the boys were with their dad for a couple more weeks. I definitely wanted to spend more time with Cal.

EPILOGUE

"...MOM, THEN PERI said ..." Miles continued his monologue about their day's adventure hiking on a neighboring island and seeing the volcano.

I'd been thumbing through the paper, and I'll confess the ad I was looking at made me lose track of his conversation for a moment.

I circled the ad under classes in the paper. LA had a wide variety of acting and other industry related classes available from writing groups to colleges. Today's paper had a special insert filled with fall classes.

One practically jumped off the page as I read it.

Class: *How to Write a Private Detective that Sells*
Class Manual: *How to Write a Dick by Shaun Kaufman and Colleen Collins*
Instructor: *Dick Macy*

I forced myself not to read further, but instead to concentrate on my son's conversation. "... and then we're going swimming."

"It sounds like fun. Have you and your brothers been behaving for your Dad and Peri?"

"Yeah. We have to because Dad wouldn't know how to handle us if we stepped out of line, and Peri's our age. I don't think she could yell at us if she tried."

"So, what you're saying is, I'm a great yeller?"

"If you have a skill you should own it, Mom." Miles laughed. "Do something exciting today, Mom. We know you're probably just sitting at home missing us. Go have some fun. We'll call tomorrow. Love ya."

"Love you and your brothers, too."

Do something exciting? I think I'd had enough excitement for a while. Well, at least of the solving a murder variety. In terms of kissing, I was definitely thinking about a bit more excitement there soon.

For a moment I simply sat and basked in the fact that my son said he loved me on purpose with no prompting.

It was a nice feeling.

He'd also said I should own my skills. Well, solving mysteries was one of my new, developing skills.

I looked back at the ad.

Instructor, Dick Macy.

Come on, really, Dick Macy?

A class on writing detectives. Yeah, a lot of scriptwriters here in Hollywood would probably flock to a class like that.

I wasn't a writer. But if you knew how to *write* a private detective, surely you'd learn something about being one.

It was a sign.

The next time I was in danger of going to jail for accidently cleaning a murder scene, I'd have a better idea how to find the real killer.

And frankly, knowing something about investigation would only help my ability to do background checks on new applicants.

I glanced back at the ad for the University's extension class. There was a long list of glowing recommendations by previous class participants.

> *"Dick Macy is a hell of a guy."* Colleen Collins and Shaun Kaufman, authors of How to Write a Dick: A Guide for Writing Fictional Sleuths from a Couple of Real-Life Sleuths.

I looked back at the top of the ad and realized that quote was from the authors of the book Dick used as his text.

I didn't want to write, but I was going to take this class.

It was a good place to start.

I wanted to know more about investigating. And I was going to confess to myself, if not to others, that I didn't want to know for work and or because I might someday clean another murder scene.

For the longest time I felt like I was treading water, looking for a calling.

Maybe I'd found one.

All because I'd accidently cleaned a murder scene and steamed some footprints.

Thank you for reading Steamed: A Maid in LA Mystery! I hope you enjoyed it. If you did, please help other readers find this book by writing a review.

And if you don't want to miss any new books, visit HollyJacobs. com and sign up for my newsletter!

Please Join Quincy on her next adventure: Dusted: A Maid in LA Mystery

Excerpt From
Dusted: A Maid in LA Mystery
(Book #2)

I looked in the mirror and felt nothing but... horror.
Orange?

I have never owned any orange clothes, so I must have suspected all along that orange might not be my color, but looking in the mirror, I was positive—orange was soooo not my color.

Frankly, I don't know that orange is anyone's color. I mean, Tiny could keep calling it *rustic pumpkin* until the cows came home, but the fact of the matter was, my maid-of-honor dress was orange.

The other fact of the matter was, I looked like giant pumpkin.

"Quincy Mac, you are absolutely stunning." Tiny's voice was all breathless wonder.

The last two weeks she'd gone from wedding-itis to full blown wedding-fever. Everything she said was breathless.

Breathless wonder.

Breathless excitement.

Breathless anticipation.

"Breathe, Tiny," I reminded helpfully as I had countless times the last few weeks.

"You look so..." She stared to cry.

Breathless and crying. Those were Tiny's two modes of communication as her wedding day drew nearer.

I filled in the blank while I waited for her to compose herself.

You look so... *much like a pumpkin.*

You look so... *scary.*

You look so... *much like a tangerine.* Oh, who was I kidding, I was no tiny tangerine. I was a full-on navel orange.

I sucked in my baby-pooch and wished I'd thought to bring my body-sucker. Oh, I know that's not what it's actually called. These days people call them by their name brand. My Grandma Mac called hers a girdle and I don't think I ever saw her without it on. I'm pretty sure she was buried in it.

Note to my boys who would some day be in charge of burying me. Do not bury me in a body sucker.

"...so beautiful," Tiny finally managed.

I smiled and put all of Mr. Magee's acting classes to use by assuring her, "I love it, Tiny."

I didn't love it, but she did and that's all that mattered. Too many people forget that a wedding is the bride and groom's special day. It's the one day when thinking about yourself isn't the least bit selfish. If she wanted me to look like a pumpkin, then by gosh, I'd be a smiling pumpkin as I walked up that aisle.

Tiny's wedding was three weeks away. I had promised myself I'd do everything in my power to be sure it was perfect.

Heck, I'd even found out who murdered Mr. Banning in order to see to it I wasn't in jail for Tiny's wedding.

Okay, truth was, I didn't want to be in jail period. And since I'd accidently cleaned Mr. Banning's murder scene, I was the only viable suspect.

Yeah, that's right. I cleaned it. I washed and polished the murder weapon. I even steamed the footprints off the carpet.

My Uncle Bill went to jail for a crime he didn't commit. Eventually the authorities realized he was innocent. They let him out of prison, but he came out with a tattoo. Mac's do not get tattoos. Or go to prison for that matter.

I was determined not to go to jail and leave my boys, or miss Tiny's wedding... or get a tattoo. I just didn't think a tattoo would age well. I was thirty-eight, and though I avoided the sun as if I were a vampire rather than simply a fair-skinned woman, I knew that wrinkles would be forth-coming. And who wants to see a wrinkled tattoo unicorn, even if it was a declaration of my innocence?

No one, that's who.

Thankfully, I found the murderer. Of course, he tried to kill me to keep me quiet, but I grew up with brothers and three sons. I kicked him and made it count. I rescued myself before Cal came in to rescue me.

Detective Cal Parker, my new boyfriend. It felt so odd to use the word *boyfriend* when I was the mother of three teens and almost forty (sigh) but I hadn't come up with any better designation for him.

I must have sighed as I thought about my cute, hunky new boyfriend because Tiny laughed. "You're thinking about him, aren't you?"

"Him, who?" I asked, trying to sound as if I didn't have a clue what she was talking about.

"Him—Detective Sexy."

"I was thinking about your wedding."

Tiny laughed some more and humphed me in a way that I knew meant she wasn't buying it.

The phone rang. I sucked in my stomach as I walked across the room in my pumpkin colored dress. I picked up the phone. "Mac'Cleaners. We do it all and we're glad you called. How may I help you today?"

"Quincy, it's me," a woman's voice said.

I didn't need any more than that to know it was Theresa Maxwell. She was officially the worst employee Mac'Cleaners had ever had. To be honest, that whole clean-ing-Mr.-Banning's-murder scene was her fault because she was supposed to be the one cleaning the dead-body house that day, but she'd called in sick. When an employee calls in sick, Tiny and I—as the business owners—step in and fill in for them. So Theresa is why I'd almost ended up in jail for a murder I didn't commit.

Theresa really was the worst employee ever, not just in an almost-sent-me-to-jail sort of way.

I'd like to fire her. I'd threatened to do just that, but I kept hoping she'd get better. Seriously, she couldn't get any worse. Although this call didn't bode well for the getting better and seemed to be pointing to worse. There was panic in her voice.

"What's up, Theresa?" I asked suspiciously.

"It's not what's up, it's what's down. I was dusting a painting at the Gifford's house and it fell. There's a tear in it now."

I'd seen the Gifford's house when I cleaned for Theresa a month ago. The last call of the day had been the dead body house, but the Gifford's house was part of her morning calls, which became my morning call when Theresa called in sick. I did not know much about art, but I knew enough to know their art was expensive. The Giffords lived in Hollywood Hills, an expensive part of town. I lived in Van George, where the cost of the houses sent my Pennsylvanian family into heart palpitations, but here in southern California was actually a mid-middle class sort of price.

"Oh…" I searched for a curse word I could use without being too crass or offending anyone. With three teenaged boys in the house, I really tried to watch myself.

"Boogers," I opted for. It was a pretty perfect curse word. Gross enough to get some umph out of, but not really offensive.

"I'm so sorry, Quincy," Theresa said. "I don't know what to do now."

"You'll have to call the Giffords and let them know what happened. Please take a picture of the damage with your cellphone, just to cross all our t's. I'll dot our i's by calling our insurance company to make a report. We've never had an accident like this happen, but please assure the Giffords we'll make it right."

"Okay," Theresa said and hung up.

I hit end on my phone and thumbed over to my contact list to look for our insurance company's number.

"Problems?" Tiny asked.

"Theresa," I managed.

"We're going to have to fire that girl," we said in sync.

I called the insurance company...

*Check out Book #2, **Dusted: A Maid in LA Mystery***

Quincy's taking classes on writing and working on a script. She's taking care of her boys, wearing a pumpkin orange maid of honor dress for Tiny's wedding, and oh... she's got another case. Someone stole Mac'Cleaner clients' artwork, and Quincy's employee is under suspicion. This is one LA maid who's got a lot on her plate in Holly Jacobs' second Maid in LA Mystery, Dusted.

The read Quincy's holiday adventure, SPRUCED UP: A Maid in LA novella!

Bio

A ward-winning author Holly Jacobs has almost three million books in print worldwide. The first novel in her Everything But… series, *Everything But a Groom*, was named one of 2008's Best Romances by Booklist, and her books have been honored with many other accolades. She lives in Erie, Pennsylvania, with her husband and four children and two dogs, Ethel Merman and Ella Fitzgerald. You can visit her at http://www.HollyJacobs.com.

ALSO BY HOLLY JACOBS:

Romance+ Stories
Just One Thing
Same Time Next Summer
Her Second-Chance Family
Words of the Heart Series
Carry Her Heart
These Three Words
Hold Her Heart

Romantic Comedies
I Waxed My Legs for This?
A Day Late and a Bride Short
Bosom Buddies
Cinderella Wore Tennis Shoes

Cupid Falls
Christmas in Cupid Falls
A Simple Heart: A Cupid Falls Novella

Short Stories and Novellas
Able to Love Again
Labor Day
There He Was
13 Weeks

Nothing But Short Story Series:
Nothing But Love
Nothing But Heart
Nothing But Luck
Rather than buy them individually, try:
Short Stories for the Overworked and Under-Read Anthology

Maid in LA Series:
My first mystery series!!
Steamed: A Maid in LA Mystery
Dusted: A Maid in LA Mystery
Spruced Up: A Maid in LA Novella
Swept Up: A Maid in LA Mystery
All four books in one edition
Maid in LA Mysteries bundle

Perry Square Series:
Do You Hear What I Hear?
A Day Late and a Bride Short
Dad Today, Groom Tomorrow
Be My Baby
Once Upon a Princess
Once Upon a Prince
Once Upon a King
Here With Me

Everything But ... Series:
Everything But a Groom
Everything But a Bride
Everything But a Wedding
Everything But a Christmas Eve
Everything But a Mother
Everything But a Dog

WLVH Series:
Pickup Lines
Lovehandles
Night Calls
Laugh Lines

Whedon Series:
Unexpected Gifts
A One-of-a-Kind Family
Homecoming Day
A Father's Name

Valley Ridge Series:
You Are Invited … *A Valley Ridge Wedding*
April Showers, *A Valley Ridge Wedding*
A Walk Down the Aisle, *A Valley Ridge Wedding*
A Valley Ridge Christmas

www.ingramcontent.com/pod-product-compliance
Lightning Source LLC
Chambersburg PA
CBHW051959220626
47052CB00004B/1016